"Did Santa bring me a prince for Christmas?" Tessie whispered as she peered down at the stranger.

Renee blinked. "No, sweetheart. He's not a present."

Her daughter had longed to meet a prince since the night of her first bedtime fairy tale. Renee had tried to tell her that those kinds of princes did not exist. And, if they did, they didn't go calling on bunkhouse cooks and their little girls. But Tessie never quite believed her.

"But what if he is a prince?" Tessie stepped closer to the phone and asked the operator. Then she turned her back, no doubt hoping Renee couldn't hear, and whispered, "Mommy doesn't know what a prince even looks like."

"That's not true—" Renee began and then stopped. She wasn't going to get into a ridiculous argument like this. Renee intended to keep her daughter safe from strange men even if Tessie was angry about it. Her daughter could afford to fall in love with fairy-tale princes, but Renee could not.

Books by Janet Tronstad

Love Inspired

*An Angel for Dry Creek
*A Gentleman for Dry Creek
*A Bride for Dry Creek
*A Rich Man for Dry Creek
*A Hero for Dry Creek
*A Baby for Dry Creek
*A Dry Creek Christmas
*Sugar Plums for Dry Creek
*At Home in Dry Creek
†The Sisterhood of the
  Dropped Stitches
*A Match Made in Dry Creek
*Shepherds Abiding in
  Dry Creek
†A Dropped Stitches Christmas
*Dry Creek Sweethearts
†A Heart for the
  Dropped Stitches
*A Dry Creek Courtship
*Snowbound in Dry Creek
†A Dropped Stitches Wedding
*Small-Town Brides
  "A Dry Creek Wedding"
*Silent Night in Dry Creek
*Wife Wanted in Dry Creek
  Doctor Right

*Small-Town Moms
  "A Dry Creek Family"
**Sleigh Bells for Dry Creek
**Lilac Wedding in Dry Creek
**Wildflower Bride in
  Dry Creek
**Second Chance in
  Dry Creek
**White Christmas in Dry Creek

Love Inspired Historical

*Calico Christmas at
  Dry Creek
*Mistletoe Courtship
  "Christmas Bells for
  Dry Creek"
*Mail-Order Christmas Brides
  "Christmas Stars for
  Dry Creek"
*Mail-Order Holiday Brides
  "Snowflakes for Dry Creek"

*Dry Creek
†Dropped Stitches
**Return to Dry Creek

JANET TRONSTAD

grew up on her family's farm in central Montana and now lives in Pasadena, California, where she is always at work on her next book. She has written more than thirty books, many of them set in the fictitious town of Dry Creek, Montana, where the men spend the winters gathered around the potbellied stove in the hardware store and the women make jelly in the fall.

White Christmas in Dry Creek

Janet Tronstad

™ LOVE INSPIRED BOOKS

Recycling programs
for this product may
not exist in your area.

ISBN-13: 978-0-373-87842-0

WHITE CHRISTMAS IN DRY CREEK

Copyright © 2013 by Janet Tronstad

www.Harlequin.com

Printed in U.S.A.

Be not forgetful to entertain strangers, for thereby some have entertained angels unawares.
—*Hebrews* 13:2

I am grateful for the many who prayed for my sister, Margaret, when she was ill with cancer. She is now dancing in heaven with Jesus, but your prayers made her feel so loved here on earth. Thank you.

Chapter One

A blizzard swept across the empty fields outside of Dry Creek, Montana, freezing the night air and throwing snowflakes against the two-story house that stood in the middle of the sprawling Elkton cattle ranch. Inside the home, Renee Gray knelt on the hardwood floor, one hand gripping a phone and the other frantically searching for a pulse in the neck of the unconscious stranger lying in front of her. She was still in shock at finding him slumped over the porch railing a few seconds ago, a saddled horse close to him and what looked like a wolf barely visible some yards behind him in the falling snow.

The wolf hadn't looked menacing, but the man did.

After the scary times she and her five-year-old daughter, Tessie, had endured with her ex-husband, Renee had been careful not to let any man who looked like this one—virile, strong and maybe dangerous—into their lives. And yet, here he was right on the floor in front of her and in desperate need of help.

With relief, she found his heartbeat. It was weak but steady. She'd already called 911 and the operator was off-line connecting with the ambulance company, so Renee relaxed enough to glance over at Tessie. It was past the girl's bedtime, but she didn't show any sign of fatigue as she leaned over the strange man protectively, her frail frame trembling with excitement.

"Is he a prince?" Tessie whispered in awe as she peered down at him. She wore cardboard angel wings on her shoulders and one of them tipped precariously. That didn't stop Tessie from reaching out to the black hair that curled against the man's forehead. Equally dark stubble covered his face. His skin was so white from cold that it almost matched the color of her wings. "Did Santa bring him for Christmas?"

Renee blinked. "No, sweetheart. He's not a present."

The two of them had been in the living room putting the last of the tinsel on their Christmas tree when the girl insisted she heard a thump outside. They both went to the door and Renee managed to use a rug to drag the man inside while keeping a watch on the darkness to be sure the wolf was gone.

"Don't touch him," Renee added as she covered the phone with her hand.

Tessie pulled back and nodded, but she kept looking at the man—particularly at the brown mole high on his left cheek.

Her daughter had longed to meet a prince since the night of her first bedtime fairy tale. Renee had tried to tell her that those kinds of princes did not exist, and if they did, they didn't go calling on bunkhouse cooks and their little girls. But Tessie never quite believed her. Renee had a sinking feeling that she knew what

Tessie had whispered in Santa's ear at the school program last week.

Renee couldn't help but stare at the man. Snow was melting in his hair. Except for the dark circles under his eyes and a faded scar on one cheek, she had to admit he did bear a striking resemblance to the drawings of the aristocratic hero in her daughter's beloved Sleeping Beauty story—especially because the prince in the book also had a mole high on his left cheek.

The temperature gauge on the porch read below zero, so Renee hadn't really had a choice about bringing the man inside, especially with that wolf following him. But she fervently hoped he would be taken away soon. She had enough trouble with Tessie's imagination without this kind of a coincidence.

Right then, the snap of chewing gum sounded in Renee's ear, indicating that Betty Longe, the 911 operator, had finished contacting the emergency crew and was back on the line.

"Is he still breathing?" the woman asked.

Renee nodded.

Then she realized the operator could not see the action. "Yes, his pulse and breathing are much better. I think it helps that he's out of the cold. The bleeding seems to have stopped, too, now that he's not moving around."

"We can ease up a bit, then. The sheriff should be there in a few minutes."

"The man needs an ambulance more than the sheriff!" Renee could hear the tension in her voice. Even though the man was doing better, she didn't have much beyond iodine and bandages to use if his wound decided to bleed some more.

Betty grunted. "Anytime a strange man stumbles onto your porch in the middle of the night with a bullet in his shoulder, I'm going to send out the sheriff along with an ambulance. Sheriff Wall is just closer than the others right now."

"Actually, we're not at my place." Renee realized that in the rush of things she hadn't mentioned that pertinent fact to the operator. She'd barely had enough wits about her to make the call. "I'm housesitting. The Elktons are spending Christmas in Washington, D.C., with their son and they asked me to stay in the main house while they're gone."

Everyone knew the bunkhouse cook at the ranch had her own quarters, and the EMTs would lose precious time if they went there first.

"Worried about possible rustlers, are they?" Betty asked, her words slow and chatty, as if she had all the time in the world.

"Yes." Renee recognized that the operator was trying to help her calm down. She took a deep breath. "Have there been more cattle reported missing?"

Betty was silent for a moment, likely passing along the additional information about where to go and then coming back to speak.

"Not that I know of. It's still seventy-three reported gone."

Renee listened for the sheriff's siren but didn't hear anything but the slight scraping sound of Tessie's slippers as she fidgeted.

"Well, be careful," Betty finally said. "Women tend

to think an unconscious man is harmless, but you never know."

"I don't think he's harmless," Renee protested. She looked down at the man. He was still breathing okay. She didn't easily trust the men she knew, let alone someone she'd never met. "I wonder what he was doing out there all alone in the middle of the night. Riding a horse and being trailed by a wolf. I can't believe he was up to any good."

"We don't have wolves around here," Betty said sharply and then paused. "Well, not many."

"It only takes one to do damage."

Renee looked up and suddenly noticed the room had grown silent. Her daughter was standing stiffly next to the man. It was as if Tessie had never danced in delight at finding the stranger. Instead, her little face was scrunched up in resignation. And the angel wings that their friend Karyn McNab had lent her to wear in the church nativity pageant seemed to weigh down her shoulders.

"What's wrong, sweetheart?" Renee asked as she covered the phone again.

"You think he's a bad man," Tessie muttered. "You don't believe Santa sent him."

"Oh, dear," Renee said to her daughter. "I know you want him to be a prince, but we talked about this. Princes don't exist. Not the fairy-tale kind, anyway. We need to accept that. And Santa is just for fun."

Tessie got a stubborn look on her face. Her lower lip protruded and her lips pressed together in a straight line. Renee would have said more, but she saw tears start to form in Tessie's eyes.

"I know who he is," the girl finally whispered. "If Santa didn't send him, then Daddy did. The prince has a Christmas message for me. He just needs to wake up so he can tell me what it is."

"Oh, sweetie," Renee said, not caring that her hand had slipped off the phone.

Before she could say anything more, Betty spoke. "Well, if you ask me, no one needs a prince like that to deliver a message. Not when we have the good old U.S. Postal Service with their white trucks and pretty stamps."

"Did you hear that, Tessie?" Renee held the phone out so her daughter could listen. She was surprised at the support she was getting from Betty, but she was grateful anyway. Maybe her daughter would pay more attention to another adult. "Betty doesn't think you need a prince, either. If your daddy wanted to write you a letter, he'd just send it in the regular mail."

Renee supposed adding some reality to her daughter's fantasies was an improvement even if the odds of Tessie's father sending her a letter were no greater than her meeting a storybook prince out here in the middle of the Montana plains.

"You listen to your mother, Tessie," Betty said, the words coming through loud enough to be heard by both Renee and her daughter. "A letter is easy enough to send."

Tessie stepped closer to the phone and asked the operator, "But what if he *is* a prince?" Then she turned her back, no doubt hoping Renee couldn't hear, and whispered, "Mommy doesn't know what a prince even looks like."

"That's not true—" Renee began and then stopped. She wasn't going to get into a ridiculous argument like this. Renee intended to keep her daughter safe from strange men even if Tessie was angry about it. Her daughter could afford to fall in love with fairy-tale princes, but Renee could not.

They were all silent for a moment.

"Maybe your mommy just hasn't met the right prince yet," Betty finally said softly, obviously changing sides before the battle had even begun.

Renee put the phone back to her own ear and whispered into it, "You're not helping."

"Well, you must admit you don't even look at single men anymore," Betty replied. "You're twenty-four years old—too young to give up on men because of one bad experience. It wouldn't hurt you to think there was a prince somewhere who was meant for you."

Without thinking, Renee let her eyes stray to the man's left hand and noticed he wasn't wearing a wedding ring. Of course, her ex-husband had seldom worn one, either, so that didn't prove much.

"I agree you don't want another man like that husband you used to have." Betty's voice had gentled again and her gum chewing had stopped. "Why, he almost took you to prison with him. And the armed robberies he committed weren't the worst of it. Everyone knows he was abusive to you and Tessie."

"I—" Renee wished she hadn't brought up her marriage. She cupped the phone to her ear so her daughter wouldn't hear. Tessie had turned around and was looking at her.

"But you can't judge all men by him." The operator

continued as though Renee hadn't even tried to speak. "There are dozens of men around here who would be happy to be a little girl's prince. And yours, too, if you'd let them. Maybe the new man who is delivering the mail in Dry Creek these days would do. He's single and has a steady job."

"Barry Grover?" Renee asked, momentarily stunned. She'd met him. He was balding and had a paunch. She looked up to see if there was a red patrol light reflecting in the window. Barry was missing a tooth, too, if she remembered right. *Sheriff Wall should be here by now. Please, Lord, bring the lawman soon,* she prayed. If she stayed on the phone with Betty much longer, all the people in Dry Creek would be out looking for a husband for her, and she was afraid of what kind of man they'd find.

It was bad enough that young Karyn, a high school student who worked weekends for her as a relief cook, had started dropping hints that marriage was good at any age. Of course, that was likely for her own benefit, since Karyn was infatuated with that boy she was seeing. Neither one of them was of an age to be thinking about a wedding, in Renee's opinion.

"Barry might be a little older than you," Betty acknowledged. "But twenty years' difference isn't so much in a marriage. And he has that nice new Jeep. It has heated seats, I hear. And four-wheel drive. He's taking some treatment for his hair loss, too, so he'll look younger before you know it. And he'll have a good retirement if he stays with the postal service. You'll be well set in your golden years. And Tessie might get that puppy she wants."

"That's okay. No one needs to match me with anyone. And I'm working on the puppy."

Renee looked back at the man on the floor. His skin color was returning to normal. He might look better than Barry Grover, but he would be more difficult. She didn't know how she knew, but she was sure of that. He just seemed like the kind of man who could turn someone's life upside down without even trying.

"We have to do it for Tessie," Betty said then, her voice thick with emotion. "Why, even before she said what she did when she was on Santa's knee, she's always been going on about—ah—" the operator hesitated and lowered her voice "—family things."

Mercifully, she stopped at that.

"I am thinking of Tessie," Renee whispered. The knot of misery in her stomach tightened. She supposed the whole town of Dry Creek knew about her daughter's stories by now.

Against all odds, Tessie still loved her father and told anyone who would listen how wonderful he was. Instead of his being an inmate in the state prison in Deer Lodge, she had convinced herself that her father had been sent on a secret mission to rule some faraway kingdom, living in a majestic castle with guards at the gate and princes at the ready. It was straight out of one of her fairy-tale books. Tessie would describe the man's crown and robes and the presents he was going to send to her. She even mentioned the wolfhounds that guarded the bridge over the moat by name.

Renee renewed her commitment to finding a suitable puppy for Tessie.

"I'm sorry. I don't mean to pry," Betty finally said,

sounding as discouraged as Renee felt. "It's just with her father the way he is—"

"I know you mean well." In a small town, no one carried his or her burdens alone. Sometimes that was good, sometimes bad. But Renee knew the concerns were as much for Tessie as they were for her, and she couldn't fault the town for caring.

She had been taking her daughter to a therapist in Billings and the woman said that Tessie would outgrow these fantasies when she finally felt completely safe. The girl's love for her father warred against her fear of him. She yearned to see him and, at the same time, was scared he might come back with some wolfhounds to hurt her. Her fairy-tale pretense of a father as a faraway king helped her feel secure until she could finally admit it wasn't the animals but her father who made her afraid.

Renee felt a chill just thinking what the sight of that wolf might do to her daughter if it came closer. Hopefully, it had already gone now that there wasn't a wounded man out there waiting to become the wolf's prey. There were no young calves or chickens around this time of year, either, but she'd still call over to the bunkhouse when she had a minute and alert the ranch hands.

"Tessie, sweetheart, maybe you should go sit in the bedroom and wait for me," Renee said with a nod to the girl.

"Good thinking," the operator said, her voice back to normal. "That little one doesn't need to be mixed up in something like this."

Tessie stood, her white-and-pink nightgown damp

from the snow that had fallen on her when she'd held the door open earlier. Her blond hair curved around her face, and her eyes were serious as she continued to look down at her prince. "I think he's smiling at me."

Renee turned her attention back to the man and eyed him suspiciously. "That's not a smile, sweetie. He's just moving his lips—maybe from the pain. He probably doesn't even know how to smile."

Tessie's eyes filled with sympathy, but she didn't back away from him.

Renee noted her daughter's eyes seemed to always return to that mole on the man's cheek. She suddenly wondered if the man could stay around long enough to show Tessie that he was no prince. It wouldn't take more than a few minutes for the man to open his mouth and prove he was mortal. Maybe that would be the first step in Tessie facing her fears and fantasies. If so, God might have sent the man for that very purpose.

"The man's moving!" the operator echoed in alarm. "I'll tell Sheriff Wall to hurry. Not that he isn't already driving as fast as he can in the snow. He'll be there soon."

"We'll be fine," Renee said, as much to reassure herself as the operator. The man's breathing had improved, but he wouldn't have the strength to do any real damage. Not with her here.

"Did you check to see if your prince has a gun?" Betty asked.

"No!" Renee gasped at her oversight and then turned to see her daughter still staring at the stranger in speculation. His lips were moving again.

Renee hated guns. And if the man was involved in

rustling, he likely had one. She put down the phone and braced herself to touch him again.

In the meantime, Tessie leaned closer.

"You can watch television in the bedroom," Renee said, promising a rare treat. "Turn the Disney Channel on. They have that princess show you like so much."

Tessie looked down at the man, clearly reluctant to leave.

"Please, sweetheart," Renee said. "Mommy needs you to go."

Tessie nodded and headed down the hallway.

"Close the door." Renee waited until Tessie did so, shutting herself in the bedroom.

Renee turned her attention back to the man. He wasn't moving his lips anymore, so she gingerly opened his wool-lined jacket. His gray flannel shirt had a large damp spot where his wound had bled and the whole garment was plastered to his chest. She didn't see any bulges that would indicate a shoulder holster, though. Of course, she knew from her ex-husband that there were many places to hide a gun if a man didn't want it to be seen. She ran her hands down the sides of his torso. The man flinched and moaned. At one point, she wondered if she didn't feel something taped to his chest. She wasn't taking any chances, so she unbuttoned his shirt and opened it.

"Oh, my," she gasped softly as she reached out to touch a bandage that stretched across the man's bare midriff. Nothing was hidden there, but he had faded red burn scars and dark bruises all over. They were not recent, but there were so many. She let a finger trail across his skin, wondering what trouble he'd seen—or caused—in his life to end up with all of these.

She felt a tremor race through her, making her hand shake slightly. His skin, while bruised, was baby soft. She pulled her hand away quickly and then pulled his shirt back together. She knew what bruises like that might mean and it frightened her. It wasn't right looking at him when he was not aware enough to stop her, though. His scars were his own business. And maybe the sheriff's.

She picked the phone up again.

"I think he's been beaten," she said to Betty. "Maybe he really is a criminal. Or maybe he tried to go straight and this is what the others did to him."

"Don't go feeling sorry for him, now," Betty advised, her voice low and serious. "Finish searching him before he comes to. And keep the phone close to you."

Renee reached for his pockets. A man like this could have a knife, too.

All she found was a scrap of paper in the front pocket of his jeans that had a smudged telephone number written on it in pencil. The melting snow had made the marks practically illegible.

His breathing became more labored as she knelt there.

"Easy, now," she said in a soothing voice as she turned the paper over. The front was a receipt for a hamburger and a cup of coffee. She couldn't make out the name of the business where he'd bought the food. She set the paper aside to give to the sheriff when he came. Maybe the phone number would be a contact for the man's next of kin.

His eyes had been closed when she found the paper, but his eyelids were twitching now. And a muscle along his jaw was clenching. Then he groaned.

Renee spoke into the phone again. "He's regaining consciousness."

"Did you find a gun?" Betty asked.

"No."

Renee heard a siren in the distance and realized the sheriff was close. She wondered if the man heard the sound. If he did, he didn't react. Her ex-husband had always flinched when he heard a cop's siren, even if he wasn't doing anything illegal at the time.

Then the man's eyes fluttered open.

"You look like an angel." His words slurred and a small, lopsided grin started to form.

"I know karate," Renee announced.

"Now, why doesn't that surprise me?" the man said, his grin spreading.

She realized then that he must have seen Tessie's angel wings. He likely hadn't realized Tessie was a different person, but he had glimpsed the wings even in the condition he was in. They'd repaired one of them earlier tonight, replacing the gold glitter border.

Renee felt her knees grow weak. She'd do anything to protect her daughter. A blast of cold air hit her neck and she turned to see that the sheriff had stepped into the room. She hadn't locked the door after she brought the stranger inside. Now she was relieved someone was here to take him away. She and Tessie didn't need this man around. Even if he was not a rustler, he wasn't safe. The quiver in her stomach told her that much.

She was still breathless from touching the bruises on his chest. This man was trouble.

Rusty Calhoun just lay there and looked at the angel kneeling beside him. She looked stressed, but in a vague, delicate way. He'd had concussions before in the eight years he'd spent in the army and he'd seen his share of hallucinations, but nothing like this. The woman's skin was so translucent it looked like a white South Seas pearl—the expensive kind. Her hair floated around her like a halo. Sometimes, when she moved her head, a speck of gold would fall from her like a star coming down to earth. He took that as a sign from the heavens that she wasn't real.

"You're the most beautiful woman I've ever seen," he finally said, deciding he could say that because she was a figment of his imagination. And a man should be able to say anything he wanted to a vision he'd created in his own mind.

The woman made a dismissive sound, but he didn't care. Not when her skin shone the way it did. It made sense that any hallucination he had would look like a pearl. His mother had loved pearls. And his nightmares in Afghanistan had been littered with them.

When he'd rambled on about a pearl necklace in his delirium on that awful night when his platoon had been bombed in the Wardak Province, the doctors searched through his belongings until they found the strand he carried with him. When they gave it to him, he'd cursed and thrown it across the room. That was when they'd called in the chaplain.

"Are you awake?" the woman asked now.

Rusty barely had time to wonder if he should answer his hallucination before a lawman took her place. Or was it two lawmen? Rusty wasn't sure. But he figured whether they were one or two, they were real enough.

"He's awake," the lawman said with authority and the two images of him slowly merged into one. "Tell me your name."

"U.S. Army ranger Rusty Calhoun, sir."

"What happened?"

The clipped voice of command sounded familiar. Voices like this had demanded his report when he had been returned to safety that dark night in Afghanistan.

"I was the only one left." The medics had pulled him out of the rubble. He hadn't wanted to leave. Not with the others lying around him.

"Who else was with you?" the voice asked.

"My platoon. The eleventh mountain division, sir. It was a trap."

There was silence after that. Rusty closed his eyes and saw the flashes of the bombs. He'd failed them all.

"Tonight?" The man's voice had softened, but it was persistent. "Here in Montana?"

Rusty felt the pounding in his head and opened his eyes. He remembered the snow now.

"Where am I?" he asked.

He smelled Christmas. The scent of pine trees and popcorn.

The doctors hadn't wanted to release him yet, but his younger brother, Eric, had called to say he needed him. Rusty had let down so many people already that he was determined to save his brother from whatever trouble he was in. The doctors said they wouldn't release Rusty until next week, but he had pressed them and left early. He hadn't called Eric and told him that he was here, though.

"You're in Montana, son. You were out riding a horse—"

"Annie. Is she all right? And my dog?"

"There was no dog," the woman said. "Maybe the wolf chased it off."

"Not a wolf. It's my dog."

"Goodness," the woman gasped.

"I—" Rusty paused. His felt sweat on his forehead, but it was cold. He'd picked up Annie and the dog from the Morgan ranch this afternoon. After his family lost the ranch, he'd paid the Morgans to board his horse and dog along with his brother until he could get back here.

"Take a minute. Think about tonight," the man's voice urged.

Rusty took a ragged breath and offered up a prayer for strength. Thanks to that chaplain, he and God had forged a truce of sorts in Afghanistan. Rusty wasn't sure the connection was going to hold in Montana, but he wasn't ready to give it up, either.

"There was a pickup." Rusty forced his mind to leave the old battles and remember the past few hours. The wind had been frigid, but he'd welcomed the bite of the snow as it hit his face.

He'd been riding on the south section of his family's ranch. His father had died while he was overseas, and riding on the land was the only way Rusty knew to say goodbye to the man. He'd been out for hours and was ready to turn back when a large black pickup seemed to emerge from the night as it came across the fields.

The pickup went off-road and into a ravine. When Rusty rode to the top of the ravine and looked down, he saw another pickup was already parked at the bottom, sitting there with its lights off. Someone stepped out of the smaller pickup, leaving the door open. The small overhead light let Rusty see enough. He knew it was Eric standing there because the boy was wearing his brown baseball cap backward. It was unlikely anyone else around here would wear a cap like that, especially when the wind was so strong.

"They shot me," Rusty added, remembering that much from his scramble up the side of the ravine. "It hurts pretty bad."

He'd signaled his dog to stay silent so it wouldn't be shot and the animal had obeyed. Rusty marveled that even though he had been gone so long, his dog still saw him as master. They'd been through some tough times together, he and that dog.

"Who shot you?" the sheriff asked as he took a small notebook out of his pocket.

Rusty hesitated. "I don't know." Fearing that might not be enough, he added, "It was too dark to see any faces."

He waited for the accusation to come. He had never lied—not even by withholding information. Until now. He knew he'd seen Eric tonight even though he hadn't seen his face. And he wasn't willing to give up his brother that easily. Not until he heard the other side of things.

The sheriff didn't press and Rusty breathed deep. Maybe the doctors were right that he merely needed some rest.

He turned to search for the woman's face. If the lawman's voice was real, she must be, too.

Just then he heard the soft sounds of slippers on the hardwood floor and he saw the woman turn to look behind her. She had a lovely neck, he thought with a smile.

"No," the woman whispered in horror as she looked at something.

Rusty tried to raise himself up to defend her from whatever was coming, but he had no strength. Then he saw the woman was merely worried about the girl who ran from behind her and stood in front of him with her little hands on her hips. Her angel wings were crooked, but her face was beaming.

"Have you seen my daddy?" she demanded to know.

Rusty felt as if the room was spinning. "What's he look like?"

He'd known too many fathers who had died in Afghanistan. "Was he an army man? In my platoon?"

"No, he's a king," the girl replied proudly as she stepped a little closer.

"British?"

"No, he's a king in Montana," she insisted with a guilty look at her mother. Then she leaned forward and whispered, "With a crown. My mommy doesn't believe, but—"

Rusty smiled, finally realizing she was pretending. He had no idea that kind of innocence was still alive anywhere in the world.

He was going to answer her when he was struck with a sudden worry. The girl must have a mortal father, too.

"Does your father wear an orange parka?"

That would describe the tall man who had been in the ravine waiting for Eric. The man must have been using night-vision goggles, too. He wouldn't have been able to see Rusty without them.

"My father always wears a purple robe," the girl said firmly. "Purple is for kings. Never orange."

He relaxed. "I haven't seen him, then."

Rusty wondered if his brother knew the man in the orange parka had taken a rifle out after the taillights on Eric's pickup disappeared from view. In the dark, Rusty wouldn't have known the man was aiming the gun at him except that he'd seen a small white beam of light a second before the shot was taken.

"Tessie, sweetheart," the woman said as she stepped forward and wrapped her arms around the girl, "the sheriff needs to ask the man some questions. And you need to go back to the bedroom."

The woman released her daughter and gave her a nudge in the direction of the hallway. All three adults watched as the girl dutifully walked down the hall and went through a door.

"Sorry about that," the woman said.

The lawman nodded and then moved closer so Rusty could see him and the notebook in his hand.

"Where were you when you got shot?"

Rusty thought a minute and then decided there was no harm in telling the lawman. "The ravine that is a quarter of a mile from the gravel road that intersects with the road that goes up to the Morgan ranch."

Rusty had been fortunate he'd been able to scramble to the top of the ravine and get on his horse before the man in the orange parka could walk over to where he had been shot.

"So you were on your father's old place? The one the bank foreclosed on?"

Rusty nodded and the slight action made him wince. "I was just looking around. No harm in that."

"An ambulance is on its way," the sheriff said as he stood up and put the notebook back into his pocket.

The sheriff had a gray Stetson on his head and it shaded his eyes, but there was no doubt where he was focused next. "I recognize you now. You were a scrawny little kid last time I saw you. That ranch of your father's was bigger than the Elkton ranch here. Got put up for sale by the bank in the past month or so. Some corporation bought it. It wasn't handled right— I'll give you and your brother that much."

Rusty tried to answer, but the pain in his head stopped him from doing more than giving a slight nod. He was surprised anyone from Dry Creek would remember him. He'd joined the army when he turned eighteen and hadn't come back until he'd gotten off the plane in Billings early this morning. That was eight long years and he'd changed.

"I keep track of your brother," the sheriff continued, his broad face looking almost sympathetic. He pushed the brim of his hat back so his eyes were no longer hidden.

Rusty nodded. "Eric is supposed to be staying with the Morgans and going to school. But they said he got temporary work on another ranch, so he wasn't there. He thinks I'm coming next week."

He heard another feminine gasp from behind his

shoulder. He tried to turn, but his shoulder twisted in pain. He could barely hear what the sheriff was saying.

"I don't know about any job, but your brother's been causing trouble," the lawman continued. "Claimed the bank cheated you all somehow. Seems your dad had a heart attack and died before he could prove he paid off the mortgage on that ranch of his. That might make your brother mad enough to steal cattle."

Rusty didn't say anything. He'd talked several times on the phone these past weeks with his brother and he had his own suspicions about what was happening around here. He knew his brother would never steal anyone's cattle. Rustling had prompted their father's need for the loan that had ultimately taken the ranch away from them all. But he feared the boy was in deeper trouble than he had thought.

"If my father says he made the payment, he did," he finally said. That much he knew for certain. His father might have been a mean, cantankerous man, but he was honest to the point of plain stubbornness.

The sheriff looked at Rusty some more, as if weighing the words Rusty was holding back as well as the few he'd spoken. Finally, the lawman squinted at the notebook in his hand. "Anyone we can contact for you, son?"

"Just my brother, Eric. He's the only family I have."

Rusty felt the sweat collecting on his forehead—which made no sense, because the air was chilly.

Another shadow flitted over him, and when he blinked, he saw the woman again. He hoped he wasn't going to pass out.

"Your brother's Eric? Eric Calhoun?" the woman demanded, clearly upset.

The woman's eyes were wide and he couldn't help but notice they were the color of warm honey with flecks of cinnamon in them.

"Yes, ma'am," he said.

"You tell your brother to stay away from Karyn McNab," the woman said with some steel in her voice. "She's too young to get married."

"Married?" Rusty repeated, stunned. "Who's getting married?"

"Your Eric wants to marry my Karyn," the woman said, the challenge obvious in her voice even before she added, "and I'm doing my best to stop them from making the worst mistake of their lives."

He looked at the woman, trying to form a reply. His mouth wouldn't work, though.

"It didn't help that Mrs. Hargrove said they could be Mary and Joseph in the church pageant," the woman added, putting her hands on her hips just as her daughter had done earlier. "They promised to come up with a donkey."

Rusty closed his eyes. He used to know a Mrs. Hargrove. But now he'd lost so much blood he must be light-headed. The odd thing was that the series of sharp pains had pushed away from him, leaving the constant dull pain behind.

"Must be some other Eric," he managed to mutter. Eric had spoken indignantly about people hinting he was involved in the cattle disappearing around Dry Creek, but he'd never said anything about a girl. "We don't have a donkey."

Of course, Rusty thought to himself, they didn't have a ranch now, either.

The woman frowned at him. "Will you tell your brother what I said?"

Suddenly, Rusty tried to answer, but hesitated and then couldn't seem to remember the question. He thought he might be going under again. He couldn't do that. Eric needed him.

Rusty took another look at the woman as he started to fall back into the darkness. She had such a sweet face, especially now that her frown was gone and she looked as if she cared whether he faded away or not.

"Look after Annie for me," he pleaded. "My horse. She's pregnant."

He wanted to see the woman again, but he couldn't find the words to say that. He wondered if she could see inside his mind and know that he was drawn to her.

"I'll do what I can," she said, her voice growing increasingly distant as he felt the room tilt.

"And my dog, too?"

Rusty tried to stay conscious to hear her answer and he thought he caught a faint echo of a yes. She might not want to do a favor for him, but he was pretty sure she would go to the aid of a pregnant animal and a dog, even one who was part wolf. He would see her again, he told himself in satisfaction as he started to drift away. Now if he could only figure out what his brother was doing.

Chapter Two

Renee stared at the man, willing his chest to rise with another breath. A thick Persian rug lay beneath him—the one she'd used to help pull him inside. It had been under the man this whole time, keeping his back warm and giving him some softness. She exhaled when she saw him inhale. She hadn't even realized she was holding her breath until then.

She wondered what kind of trouble he had known. Had it all been from Afghanistan or had he gotten some of those bruises closer to home?

Not that it was her business, she reminded herself. She braced herself and turned to the sheriff. "I suppose you're going to arrest him now?"

The man was unconscious again, so she didn't think he'd mind her asking.

"Arrest him?" The sheriff looked over in surprise. "We can't do that. Even if cattle are missing—and it looks like they are—there's no proof Rusty Calhoun has done anything wrong. It's all circumstantial."

The front door was still open, but Renee barely noticed the sting of the cold air. The snowflakes had slowed. Earlier, there had been a full moon, but the clouds had come out since then to make everything dark except where the porch light came through the windows and door of the house. The stranger's horse was standing patiently by the porch rail. The man's black Stetson had been pushed against the corner post by the wind. There was no sign of his dog.

"I didn't think you needed all that much proof around here to arrest someone," Renee finally said. She tried not to let her feelings show. "He was shot in a place where cattle are almost certainly missing. Ranchers are going out on patrol—like as not with their rifles. It's circumstantial, sure, but you didn't have that much more when you arrested me."

The sound of a distant television let her know Tessie was securely in the bedroom and would not hear them. Yet neither she nor the sheriff said anything for a good minute.

Finally, the lawman shook his head. "You still hold that against me? I don't know how many times I've explained that I arrested you for your own protection. You had been part of the theft at that gas station. We didn't know at first that you'd been forced into it by your abusive husband. A blind man could see that he was setting you up to take the fall on those armed robberies he was pulling off. Even after we picked him up, that accomplice of his was still running around free and he was dangerous. I wanted to keep you safe from him. You were never even brought to trial. And it all happened a year ago. It's not like you have a record from it or anything to hold you back."

Renee nodded, but she didn't meet the sheriff's eyes.

"I'd just never been arrested before. Not even a parking ticket."

She had no quarrel with the law. The legal system might be a little black-and-white at times, but every criminal had some sad story in his background. She'd certainly had hers. And this man wouldn't be the first wounded veteran to do something impulsive. All people needed to be held accountable for their actions. Except that she hadn't done the crime.

"I don't go around arresting people for no reason," the sheriff continued gruffly, his face turning slightly pink.

"Well, I suppose I could have done better, too." Renee had to give him that. "I didn't help my ex-husband with those robberies, but I sure didn't know how to stop him, either."

When Renee had seen that her husband was robbing gas stations, she'd finally been desperate enough to come look for her father. She'd ended up at Gracie Stone's nearby house, in as bad shape as this man was tonight.

"That doesn't make you guilty of anything," the sheriff said. "Stopping him was my job. What you should have done was come tell me what he was doing. Sooner than you did."

Renee nodded. After Gracie and her father married, they welcomed her and Tessie into their family along with Gracie's three grown sons. But Renee wouldn't let herself lean on the Stone family. She needed to find strength inside herself if she and her daughter were ever going to have a good life. Now that she was a Christian, she believed she could do that.

"I'm not saying you should arrest this man," she finally said. "It's just that if you are going to arrest the guy tonight, I want you to do it now, before Tessie has a chance to come back. She thinks he's a prince. It would break her heart to see you put handcuffs on him."

"I wouldn't do anything to hurt that little girl," Sheriff Wall responded. "You know that."

The sheriff leaned back on his haunches and continued, "And while we're on the subject, I know Tessie is not particularly comfortable with any of the men around here. Well, except for her grandfather."

"Tessie and men are—" Renee paused, searching for the right word "—complicated."

The sheriff nodded. "But she seems to really like this guy. At least enough to talk to him and call him a prince. She's not afraid of him, either. That's something for her. He needs to be checked out better, but he sounds like he's single. I wouldn't rule him out completely. For all their faults, the Calhouns were honest people. And Tessie sure needs a better father than the one she's got."

Renee turned to the lawman in astonishment.

"He's absolutely the worst kind of man we could get involved with. Look at him." She gestured. "Only a violent man gets that many wounds. He spouts all kind of romantic nonsense about angels just hoping some woman will be foolish enough to fall for it. He might have Tessie wrapped around his little finger, but I'll never budge. He and my ex-husband are enough alike to be brothers. I hope I never see him again after tonight. He even has a wolf for a dog. What kind of a father would he make for a little girl?"

"Ah," the sheriff said. "Well, that's too bad."

They were both silent again.

"You've been talking to Betty, haven't you?" Renee finally asked.

Sheriff Wall pushed his hat down farther on his head. "Betty's the dispatcher. I talk to her all the time."

Renee gave the sheriff a stern look. "Just so you know—I'm not looking for a husband. She thinks I need one. I don't. Tessie and I are doing just fine."

"Understood," the lawman said with something like relief in his voice. "I like to help, but I'm not much good as a matchmaker anyway."

"No, you're not," Renee agreed with a smile.

The sheriff was silent for a moment and then he pointed to the phone Renee held in her hand. "Speaking of Betty, is she still—"

Renee grimaced in dismay and held out the phone. She'd forgotten all about it.

The lawman took it and put it to his ear. "You still on here, Betty? Could you call Havre and see if they have anything on a Rusty Calhoun? They probably don't, but it's a place to start."

Renee could hear the ambulance as it stopped in front of the house. The sound of boots announced the arrival of two uniformed men as they came through the open doorway. The thin worker had a tattoo on his hand and the stockier one had a beard.

"This must be our patient," the tattooed man said as he knelt and put his fingers over the pulse on Rusty's throat. "He's doing better than I thought he might from what Betty said."

Renee felt relief wash over her as the two men loaded Rusty onto a gurney and wheeled him out of the house.

The sheriff hung up the phone. "They'll take Rusty to the clinic in Miles City. There's nothing for you to worry about. You and Tessie can go to bed."

"Oh, that reminds me," Renee said as she reached into her jeans pocket and pulled out the slip of paper. "I took this out of the man's pocket. It has a phone number on it."

The sheriff took the paper and studied it. "Not a local number. Looks like something back east. I'll have to give it back to him, though. No permission for a search."

"He was unconscious," Renee said.

"All the more reason." The sheriff started walking toward the open door. "If I end up arresting him for anything, it could jeopardize the whole case."

Renee could see the taillights of the ambulance through the side window on the house. A gust of cold wind blew inside before the sheriff could close the door. Renee wrapped her arms around herself. She felt the chill and shivered. She suddenly realized she'd have to see that man again. She had his horse and that beast he called a dog. She'd have to call over to the bunkhouse to see if anyone was awake to help her. She didn't want to walk out to the barn in the dark with that animal around. Just because the man called him a dog didn't make him one.

Early the next morning, Rusty sleepily noticed the antiseptic smell around him while his eyes were still closed. This place felt familiar, but he wasn't ready to wake up. It was not full light yet and he heard the rumble of voices in the distance. Slowly he remembered and his entire body tensed. He started to reach for the knife he kept in his right boot. Then he realized his toes were bare. He wore no socks. His boots were gone.

He opened his eyes and tried to rise on his elbows to look around. He had trouble because he had a bandage around his chest, and one arm was tangled up somehow. He wasn't in the humble hospital where he'd spent weeks after being wounded that last time in Afghanistan, though. The knowledge made him relax. The walls here were painted a light pink and the windows were intact. His boots were beside his bed. He slumped back against the pillows. He even smelled a hint of coffee in the distance.

A cotton blanket had been draped around him, but the air was cool. There was no hint of food and he wondered if he had missed breakfast. He had a headache, but he could easily move his left hand and reached over to the bandage on his side. His arm was in a sling. He remembered now that they'd brought him here in what seemed like the middle of the night.

He looked at the machine next to his bed and pushed the call button. The events of last night were coming back to him. He was amazed he'd headed for the Elkton ranch like a homing pigeon when he was in trouble. His mother had always said Mr. Elkton had the best ranch around. It had made his father furious, but Rusty agreed with her. He'd been ten years old when they'd first had that argument.

Now he just shook his head. He didn't have time for memories—good or bad. He was anxious to get out of here and find out what kind of trouble his brother had gotten mixed up in.

Rusty was reaching for his boots with his good arm when his eye caught a furtive action near the open door. He glanced up just in time to see a dark shape move out of view. He hadn't seen much, but he knew there was no white or pastel color on the figure, so it wasn't a nurse.

"Who is it?" he demanded, realizing why he'd flashed back to Afghanistan. Someone had almost killed him last night and he didn't know why. He could still be in danger. He'd never been as scared in his life as he had some nights in the army. He wondered if fear would always pull him back there.

He dragged his right boot close and slipped his hand down to the small pocket in the interior of the leather where he kept his knife. It was empty.

He moved to the wall beside the door anyway and lifted the boot. The heel was hard enough to knock someone out. Even clad in this threadbare hospital gown and with only one arm working, he could do enough damage to slow someone down if he had to get away.

"Rusty," someone whispered and he relaxed. He recognized that voice. He put his boot down at the same time as his angel peeked around the corner of the doorway. He hadn't realized last night that she was so slender and slight. Just a wisp of a woman.

"Are you all right?" she asked hesitantly. "The nurse said you were still sleeping."

"Not anymore." He grinned for no good reason.

Then he stopped and just looked at her. She'd been all golden and shining last night. Today she was subdued and more copper than gold. Maybe it was the difference in her hair. It wasn't spread out in a halo this morning; she'd pulled it back into a smooth braid. The hair still captured the light, but it was deeper, more intense. And her face was paler than it had been last night. But that didn't make sense. She wasn't scared of him today the way she had been then.

At least, he didn't think she was afraid today until he saw her blink. That was the exact moment she'd gotten a clear look at him.

"Someone messed with my boots," he tried to explain, hoping that would be enough to make the sight of him seem normal as he stood hunched by the wall with his hospital gown open in the back, his boot clenched to his chest and a blanket caught in the loose ties of his gown.

"Oh." She nodded uncertainly.

She had freckles on her nose. He wondered how he had missed that last night. And her face looked drawn, as if she was worried about something and had been for some time.

"How's your little girl?" he asked, realizing as he said it that the woman must be married since she had a daughter who thought her father was a king.

Not that it was any of his concern if she was married.

"Fine."

Rusty knew so little about family life. His mother had left a few months after she'd made her comments about the Elkton ranch. Then it had been Rusty, baby Eric and their father doing the best they could. It didn't take them long to forget all of her housewife ways. They ate from tin cans when they were hungry and slept in beds without sheets when they were tired. He knew boys were expected to like that kind of life, but he would have traded it all to have his mother come back to visit, even if it was just one time.

Rusty felt the weight of the blanket and looked down long enough to untangle it and wrap it around him like a toga.

"Are you Mrs. Elkton?" he asked his visitor as he then knotted the hospital gown ties around his back so everything was secure.

Mr. Elkton had been a widower when Rusty was a boy, but a lot could have changed since then.

The woman shook her head as though what he'd said was unthinkable. "I'm the cook for the ranch hands. My daughter and I live in our own place behind the bunkhouse. We're just taking care of the main house while the Elktons are gone. We don't own it or anything like that."

"Oh." Rusty was uncomfortable now that he seemed to have made the woman feel as if she was less than he had expected. Not that he knew why she felt what she did. He must look like a deranged drifter, so she shouldn't be worried about impressing him.

It was a reminder, though, of why he avoided pretty, delicate-looking woman like her. He never understood them and he'd had a few relationships where he'd tried. He preferred women who were uncomplicated. If they had any emotion, they kept it to themselves. Serviceable was what they were, he thought. Good soldiers. If he ever hooked up with a woman, it would be with one like that.

"I'm sorry," Rusty finally mumbled.

Just then a nurse sailed into the room, a clipboard in her hands and a small frown on her face. She assessed the situation in a glance. "If you're looking for that knife of yours, the sheriff took it out of your boot. We don't allow weapons in the hospital."

"Of course you don't." Rusty was more comfortable with a woman like that. The nurse was starched and disapproving, without a hair out of place. She knew how to take orders and give them. She couldn't be hurt or dismayed by anything he did.

"The sheriff also said you're free to go when we're finished with you," the nurse added.

"Thanks," Rusty said.

"You had a knife?" his visitor asked then, apparently still shocked. "All that time last night, you had a knife?"

The woman's voice rose in hysteria. She made his spine tingle. He felt an urge to promise he'd never touch a knife again, not even to cut his steak. Or butter his bread, if it came to that.

"I wasn't going to use it," he assured her as best he could. It didn't seem to do much good, if the outraged expression on her face was any indicator.

"Honestly," he added. "I left my military blade in the hospital back east and bought the kind of knife the ranch hands usually have. It's more to cut twine than hurt anyone."

She looked at him, suspicion pinching her face. "Some men have been trained to kill with a fork."

"Not me," he said, defending himself. He could kill with a ballpoint pen, but he thought it best not to mention that. "I'm finished with violence."

The chaplain had brought him that far, at least. He

wasn't prepared to gather any more guilt on his soul over people being hurt. Not even when it came to the feelings of a flighty, emotional woman like this one.

"I need to take your vitals," the nurse announced as she stopped pushing buttons on the machine by the bed. "It's best if you're lying down when I do."

"Just a minute." Rusty kept his eyes on his visitor. She wasn't looking too steady.

"My daughter was there," she finally said, as though that explained it all.

Even if he hadn't done anything to cause her distress, Rusty didn't like seeing her this way. He reached to his left and pulled a chair over for her. He was remembering more about last night the longer he stood there. Maybe he wasn't as blameless as he thought.

"I promise you were safe," he assured her. He wasn't sure how she'd react if he took her hand, but that was what he wanted to do. "I'm sure I scared you, but I would never have hurt you. I owe you my life. If you hadn't taken me into your house last night, I would have died."

He hated to say it, but he was a fair man. She deserved the acknowledgment. "I owe you big-time."

"I didn't have a choice," she said, a little downcast.

That wasn't the response he'd expected.

"Well, I'd like to think you don't regret it," he said a bit stiffly.

She finally sat down on the chair.

"No, I don't regret it," she admitted and a shy smile formed at the edge of her mouth. If he wasn't mistaken, she was teasing him. "Not too much, at least."

The morning light came in through the window and

settled around her, making her face shine a little. He could see why he'd thought her skin was the color of pearls last night.

"You truly are remarkable," he said softly.

Her honey-colored eyes widened and the specks in them seemed to multiply. She clearly hadn't expected him to be that nice.

"I'm just myself," she said.

That was why he should never forget that excitable women were completely incomprehensible to him. It wasn't as if he'd been going to lean over and kiss her or anything. She didn't need to be alarmed at a simple compliment.

And then he realized he was standing too close. She was sitting in the chair and he was leaning in a little so he could talk to her easily. Hovering, really. Maybe he would have kissed her if she kept smiling that way.

That would never do, he thought as he straightened himself.

"What I should have said is that I'll pay you for last night." He instinctively reached for his wallet. Which, of course, he didn't have since his clothes were gone. He looked over at the small table beside his hospital bed. "Don't worry. I'll write a check before you leave."

"I really should take your blood pressure," the nurse interjected. "And don't let Renee tell you that she's just a cook. She keeps that bunkhouse working. Doctors the men when they're sick. Makes them take their vitamins. Sees they call their families."

"So your name's Renee," Rusty said with a smile.

The woman gave a curt nod. "Renee Gray."

"Lovely name. I'm Rusty Cal—"

"—houn," Renee and the nurse said in unison and then laughed.

"There's no such thing as a stranger around here," the nurse finally said. "We all know your name."

"Can you give us a minute?" Rusty asked the nurse. He still wasn't certain that Renee was doing so well this morning. She was acting a little erratic, in his opinion. Scared one moment and delirious the next.

"Well, I guess I can come back later," the nurse agreed.

Rusty couldn't detect any hint of hurt feelings or dismay in the nurse's voice. Yes, she was the kind of woman for him, even if he couldn't quite picture kissing her.

"Now," Rusty said when he turned to Renee. The nurse was gone and he realized he had nothing left to say. "Oh, and I owe you for taking care of Annie, too," he suddenly remembered.

She shook her head. "Pete, one of the ranch hands, helped me. She's doing fine in the barn." She paused. "I didn't see your dog, but Pete and I left some steak bones out by the barn and they were gone this morning."

"He's around. He won't be far from Annie."

"What's his name?"

"Dog."

"He looks like a wolf."

"That's why I call him Dog. To remind people."

"Oh."

"Tell Pete thanks, too."

Rusty was going to owe a lot of people before this was all over.

"I—ah." The woman nodded and then stood up. "I

came because I called the Elktons this morning and told them what happened last night. Mr. Elkton wanted me to pass along an invitation for you to stay in the bunkhouse, if you want—with the ranch hands. Mr. Elkton said he remembered you from when you'd worked for him a few days when you were a boy."

"Really? He remembered me after all these years?" That touched him.

Renee nodded. "He said he'd never seen a kid work like you did. And all for a necklace. Wouldn't even take a break for a soda. And then you came back two extra Saturdays and chopped wood because you thought he'd overpaid you the first time."

"We Calhouns don't take charity." Rusty wouldn't have been able to buy the necklace in time if he hadn't accepted the man's extra money, though.

"Well, I hope whoever you bought those pearls for appreciated it," Renee said politely. "Mr. Elkton remembered you describing it to him. Said you talked about it being the most beautiful strand of pearls ever strung together."

"I should have taken those pearls out and buried them like Dog does his bones in the backyard," he said bitterly.

"Oh."

Renee looked at him for a bit.

"I shouldn't have said that," he finally admitted. "They were proper pearls. Still are. It's not their fault they weren't good enough."

He saw no point in stirring up past heartache. He'd bought the pearls for his mother's birthday, only to have her leave home with some guy in a pickup five hours after Rusty had given the necklace to her. She didn't even have the courage to tell his father what she was doing. She'd left when his father was out in the fields and Rusty had to tell him what happened. Rusty hadn't known his mother had left the necklace behind until he went to bed and saw it on his pillow. No note or anything with it.

They had been the best pearls Rusty could afford, but they were not good enough for her. Something in him had given up that day. Maybe that was why he never seemed to understand those pretty, delicate-looking women like his mother. He'd never tried again to please a woman—and now the same kind of soul-churning woman stood in front of him with that hesitant look on her face, clearly unsure of how she felt about him.

Putting the past behind him, he stood up, military tall. "Tell Mr. Elkton that I appreciate his offer of a place to stay."

"Well, it's just a temporary arrangement until you can get settled somewhere else," Renee added and then swallowed. "We just— He didn't know if you had anywhere to go."

"I'll do something while I'm there to earn my keep. And I'm serious when I say I want to pay you for the care you gave me last night."

"I didn't do much," the woman said with a shrug that reminded him again of his mother. They both looked as if they carried the weight of the world on their backs and were too fragile to survive. His heart always went out to women like that.

"Well, I'd still like to pay you something," he said.

Right was still right, even if he shouldn't get involved with her.

She looked at him again for a minute.

"Maybe you could do me a small favor," she finally said, biting the corner of her lips nervously.

"Of course."

"I want you to talk to my daughter."

Rusty was surprised. "I don't really have much in common with little girls."

Truthfully, he'd rather give the woman a few hundred dollars.

"Just tell her you don't have a message from her father," the woman said in a rush. "That you don't even know her father. Tell her you're not a prince."

"I guess I could do that," he said slowly. "Those things are all true."

And they were fairly obvious, he would think, even to a child.

The woman nodded. "Good, then. It's settled. Tessie is at the practice for the nativity pageant. You can come with me to pick her up."

Rusty nodded.

"Just be careful not to volunteer to play a part."

"Me?" No one had ever suggested he belonged in a pageant before. The thought was rather alarming. "I don't think I'm the type."

"Good." Renee seemed relieved. "The kids are so impressionable at that age."

"I'm sure they're all angels," he assured her, trying not to let it sting that she thought he was a danger to the children.

She laughed and left his room, much to his relief.

It took the hospital five minutes to find his clothes and another forty-five minutes to discharge him. Rusty wasn't sure Renee would still be waiting for him, but he found her in the lobby area, leafing through a magazine.

He walked toward her. "Thanks for staying."

She stood up. "Later you'll be able to share the pickups that the ranch hands drive around. But until then, I figure all you have is your horse. Unless you want to ride around on that wolf of yours."

Rusty nodded. "Dog is pretty big, all right. Thanks for looking out for him and Annie. I'll take them back to the Morgan ranch as soon as I can ride. Unless I've found a place to rent by then. And I'll ask around for a pickup to buy."

He didn't want her to think he was poor. He'd never given much thought to money when he was in the service, but he did have a good-sized savings account.

"You should wait to spend any money until you get the hospital bill," she said. "You might be amazed at how much it costs to get fixed up now that you're not in the army. I know you've had your share of hospital stays."

There was something off about the look she gave him then, as though she had a secret and it was making her blush. Why would she care about his hospitalizations, anyway? How did she even know about them?

It wasn't until he followed her outside that he figured it out.

Chapter Three

Renee opened the door to the backseat of the cab and pulled out a long-handled white scraper. Without saying anything to Rusty, she cleared her usual small hole in the ice on the windshield. She had expected him to walk around to the other side of the pickup and sit inside while she finished. After all, it was cold enough outside to see their breath and he'd just been released from the hospital.

But he stood behind her waiting, one free hand tucked in the pocket of his jacket and the other curled up in that sling.

"That's it," she informed him cheerfully after scraping the small space twice. She did it once for the ice and then again for the snowflakes that had started to fall.

"That's not enough." Rusty held out his hand. "Here. Give it to me."

"I don't see—"

He just held out his hand.

"Well, fine, then." She gave him the scraper and he took her place at the windshield. She hadn't expected him to do much with it, but he started in on the bottom corner of the windshield, scraping away until the cleared space grew larger.

"You might as well wait inside," he finally said and opened the cab door for her with his left hand. "This is going to take a few minutes."

Renee went inside and turned the heat on. She decided something was highly suspicious about this man. He'd done half of the windshield now, walked around the pickup to the other side and was still scraping so hard she thought both his shoulders must hurt. But he didn't grimace or slow down. Or look irritated. In fact, she thought she heard him whistling, low and quiet. For some reason, that reminded her of the gangster who would never walk past a cat without petting it enough to make it purr. There was something unnatural about so much goodwill in a man like him, who'd seen so much violence.

Renee refused to watch his progress, so she looked out her side window. Last night's blizzard had left a foot of snow on the ground and the tire tracks in the parking lot were deep. Fortunately, she already knew the county plow had cleared the freeway between Miles City and the Dry Creek exit, so they would be able to get through.

When Rusty finally opened the passenger door and pulled himself inside, his cheeks were red from the freezing air and a few snowflakes sparkled in his black hair. He bent down to set the scraper on the floor mat and then straightened up to rub his hand against his jeans. He might have just been warming it, but she suspected his actions meant he felt satisfied with what he'd done.

"Thank you," Renee said and looked over at him with her best fake smile. He had brushed the snow off of the hood, too. "But I could see well enough out of the little patch I cleared. You really didn't need to go to all that work."

Rusty grunted. "I certainly did if I wanted to be sure I'd live to see another day. A soldier is only as good as his equipment. What if a vehicle suddenly decides to pass on your blind side?"

"Well—" She pursed her lips and put the pickup in gear, backing out of the parking space. "People shouldn't be going that fast on these kinds of roads anyway."

Renee didn't regret the self-righteous tone in her voice. Who was he to lecture her on safety? She wasn't the one riding around at night on a pregnant horse and getting shot at, for goodness' sake.

She turned around in the clinic lot and drove to the parking exit. She looked both ways, just to show she was safety minded, and then eased the vehicle onto the main road.

"People don't always do what you'd expect," Rusty said and his voice had an element in it that hadn't been there before. It wasn't quite amusement, but it was something just as warm. "Sometimes people surprise you."

He looked at her and that was when she knew he wasn't speaking about the other drivers on the road. For the first time this morning, she felt nervous. He meant her.

"What do you mean by that?" she asked as she steered the pickup onto the freeway.

He shrugged. "Just that a man never knows."

She didn't look at him, but she could feel his eyes on her.

"If you're talking about that invitation to stay at the ranch, it came from my boss. I was only following orders." The windshield was going to need defrosting in addition to the scraping.

"It's not the invitation," Rusty said.

"Well, then?" No other vehicles were around her, so she turned to glance at him.

"You took my shirt off, didn't you?" he finally said.

She turned her eyes back to the road ahead. She could feel the embarrassment crawl up her neck and warm her cheeks. She reached over and moved the heat knob to the defrost setting. She should have known the man was difficult after all that windshield business. No one scraped the full windshield.

"And you did it while I was unconscious," the man added for emphasis, making it seem much worse than it was.

"It's not what it sounds like," Renee said as she turned onto the ramp leading to the freeway. "I was checking you for guns."

"I don't have a gun," he said, taking the same tone she had over all the unnecessary scraping he had done.

"Well, how was I supposed to know that?" Renee looked over at him in exasperation. "You had a bullet in your shoulder. Only a fool doesn't have a gun if they are going to be out there getting shot at."

There was a little slickness to the asphalt. Renee was glad there wasn't much traffic. Even that slow-moving pickup ahead of them wouldn't be a problem.

Everything was quiet in the cab.

"I know you're worried about weapons," Rusty said then. "So I forgive you."

She turned sharply to face him. "There's nothing to forgive. The police dispatcher asked me to check. It was—ah—official."

At that very moment, a burst of morning sun broke through the overcast sky above them and shone through the side window, bathing Rusty in all its glory. He'd managed to shave before leaving the hospital and he looked positively virtuous. She could hardly believe he was the same dangerous-looking man from last night. His black hair drooped softly over his forehead and the dark circles under his eyes had almost disappeared.

He turned to look at her and arched an eyebrow. "The police dispatcher asked you to take off my shirt?"

"I didn't—" Renee stammered. She suddenly remembered she had opened up his shirt after she'd looked for a gun. And Betty hadn't told her to unbutton anything. "I didn't take it all of the way off."

"That's okay." Rusty spread his fingers in a V, making the traditional peace gesture. "I already said I forgive you."

"If you would just listen," Renee said then, her temper giving her voice substance, "my only concern is that if you're going to get shot, you should have a gun! You need to defend yourself. No reason to be target practice for someone. Or can't you shoot a gun?"

Renee knew she was making no sense. She hadn't wanted him to have a gun until she realized he was in danger.

"I can shoot," he said grimly. The clouds returned and the sunlight around him fell away.

Renee should have known he'd be familiar with guns. He had been in the army, after all. Still, she'd been up half of the night thinking about what could have happened to him out there in the darkness with someone gunning for him. There were miles and miles of ranch land and only a few buildings in this part of Montana. He could have ridden around all night and not found a single inhabited house. If the man was going to take on a life of crime—and she suspected that was the case even though the sheriff hadn't found any proof yet—he needed to approach it with some common sense.

"I guess you could always get one of those vests that the police wear," she added when he didn't say anything. "I don't know where you buy them, but Sheriff Wall would know."

Rusty turned and looked at her for some time. "You're really worried about me, aren't you?"

He sounded astonished.

"Just because I don't want to see you dead doesn't mean I care," she snapped back at him in a not-so-nice way. Which made her feel bad.

"Look, I'm sorry," she said. "I've been under a lot of strain lately."

He held his hand up again with that ridiculous peace gesture. She wished he'd say something, but he just sat there.

Well, Renee told herself, this was turning into one uncomfortable drive.

She scrambled to find something else to talk about.

"Did they feed you breakfast before they let you go?"
His silence was making her feel rattled. She was only
trying to show a little human compassion. He didn't
need to be so difficult.

The best way to treat this man, she decided, was to
pretend he was nothing but another ranch hand. He was
younger than most of the men Mr. Elkton had working for him these days and certainly better-looking,
but he probably liked to eat as much as any of them.
The truth was that some of the men could spend hours
describing the perfect pancake. And then they'd start
in on the different kinds of syrups they liked to have
with their perfect pancakes.

"The nurse gave me a biscuit and some coffee,"
Rusty said without enthusiasm. "Cream for the coffee."

"Well, that's not enough," Renee protested con-
genially. In addition to talking about food, the ranch
hands loved to complain about it. "You lost a lot of
blood. They should have fried you some beef liver or
something."

"For breakfast?" he protested.

Renee nodded. "It's got lots of iron. Beets do, too."

"That doesn't mean I want beets for breakfast."

"Well, oatmeal, then—with raisins."

By the time they finished talking about what kinds
of food were appropriate for the breakfast of a man
who had been wounded and half-frozen the night before, they were turning off the freeway and heading
into Dry Creek.

There was more snow on the road now and Renee
was glad all the Elkton pickups had four-wheel drive.
She'd also chosen the one that had a back bench, so

there was lots of room for Tessie's booster seat. Her daughter didn't officially need it anymore, but she'd only just turned five and she was small for her age.

"Don't they ever change that sign instead of just repainting over the numbers?" Rusty scowled as he nodded his head toward the green metal sign that read Welcome to Dry Creek. "I think it said population one-oh-eight when I was here last. Now, eight years later, it's population one-oh-two. The two looks funny."

Renee loved that sign. In the spring, someone always planted gladiolus bulbs in the dirt beside it and the flowers bloomed in all kinds of colors for almost a month. It reminded Renee of English tea shops and elegant nurseries. Not that Dry Creek had either of those, but somehow, she told herself, they had the same spirit.

"Just because someone moves away is no reason to throw out a perfectly good sign," Renee said as she took a firmer grip on the wheel and sat up straighter in the driver's seat. "Don't know why anyone would want to leave, but some do."

"So you like it here?" he asked.

She glanced over, tempted to say it was none of his business, but he seemed interested.

"I never want to live anywhere else," she said simply as she turned her attention back to the road. "I'm building a life for me and my daughter here. It's where we belong."

Rusty nodded. "She's a good girl. Your daughter."

Tessie was with Mrs. Hargrove this morning. Renee glanced over at him again. "Don't pretend you know her—"

Just then Renee felt the pickup slide to the right.

She'd hit a patch of ice when she wasn't looking. She gripped the wheel tighter and started to twist it. She'd seen vehicles overturn on stretches like this. She felt a clutch of panic in her stomach.

What would Tessie do if something happened to her? She felt the fear slice through her. Surely her ex-husband wouldn't have custody of their daughter then. The simple divorce papers her husband had had one of his prison friends prepare—thinking to hurt Renee— had made only minimal mention of Tessie. But Renee had signed and decided she'd look into the situation about Tessie later. After all, her husband would be in prison for years, she'd told herself. They didn't have to worry about him yet.

"Let it ease its way," Rusty said as he reached over to put his left hand on the wheel, stopping her in mid-turn. "We'll be fine."

He gripped the wheel for a second and then loosened his hold.

Before Renee could protest, the slide was over and they were safely straightened out. She wasn't sure what he had done, but it had worked.

"Thank you," Renee said breathlessly. She knew an attorney who went to church in Dry Creek. She'd talk to him tomorrow. "I'm not used to driving when there's ice."

"You did fine," Rusty said. "You just need to go with the slide and not fight it. You lose all control otherwise."

She forced herself to take another breath.

It hadn't occurred to her until then that Rusty had moved over in the seat until he was right next to her so he could grab the wheel. She could feel his breath on her neck. The air was cold and she remembered she'd turned the heat down. She was going to reach for the knob and turn the heat back on, but her hands felt glued to the wheel.

Rusty put his hand on her shoulder. "You can pull off the road if you need to. It doesn't make sense to drive when you've had a scare like that."

He looked out the window. "There's a pull-off right there."

"That's the drive to the Enger place," Renee said, her teeth starting to chatter, whether from the cold or her sudden burst of nerves she didn't know. "It's not a pull-off."

"Well, it will work," Rusty insisted, his voice soothing.

Renee decided it couldn't hurt to take a minute to collect herself. She turned the wheel and drove into the turning lane for the crossroad. No one was driving down the lane this week anyway—Linda and Duane Enger had taken a trip to Hawaii. Duane was putting on a guitar workshop there and Linda had found someone to work in the café for her. They planned to spend a few days at the ocean. Renee took a moment to picture herself sitting next to them on a beach somewhere, thinking that might calm her. It didn't.

So she put the vehicle in Park.

"I'm going to leave the heater on," she informed him.

"Are you chilly?" Rusty asked and put his good arm around her shoulders, as if that was the answer to everything.

"I'm fine," Renee managed to mumble even as she

had to admit to herself that his gesture did warm her up faster than the heater ever could.

"You're experiencing a little bit of shock," Rusty said. "I've seen it many times in battle."

"You have?" Somehow his arm didn't make her feel as comforted now that she knew it was a battleground exercise for him and not a sign of—she stumbled even in her thoughts—friendly support. Yes, that was what she wanted. Friendly support. From a stranger.

She turned away, reaching toward the steering wheel. "I suppose we might as well be going."

"If you say so," Rusty said and then she felt him touch her on the back of her neck. At least, she thought he did. It was such a light brushing of his thumb across her skin that, by the time it was over, she wasn't sure if it had ever happened.

"Oh." She turned automatically.

By then the man had scooted away from her and was on the other side of the seat, looking straight ahead. She could tell by his posture that he thought he'd crossed some line.

"Did you do that to all of your troops?" she asked a little indignantly.

He looked back at her and grinned. "Do what?"

"Run your thumb across their necks."

The twinkle in his eyes made her catch her breath.

She found herself smiling. One minute he was this dangerous-looking army man and the next his eyes were as mischievous as a boy's.

She just shook her head as she put the pickup into Drive and started into Dry Creek. The snow hadn't stopped people from coming into the small town today.

Even though the owner, Linda, was on vacation, the café was open and several pickups were parked in front of it. A sign on the café announced a sausage-and-biscuit special.

On the other side of the snow-packed street, the large window in the front of the hardware store was lined with frost. Renee could see through it to where several of the older men of the area were sitting around the potbellied stove drinking their usual morning coffee.

"They look like they're arguing," Rusty observed as he stared out his window. "I always remember the men sitting there disagreeing on something or other."

"They're probably discussing who's going to be King Herod in the pageant," Renee said with a smile. "One of them has to volunteer."

"Cowards," Rusty muttered mildly.

"They all think Charlie should do it," Renee admitted. "But he says the king is bad even by heathen standards. He's afraid none of the children will look at him the same if he plays such a wicked character."

"Herod is probably just misunderstood." Rusty looked at her with a grin.

"He tried to kill the baby Jesus!"

"Oh."

They were silent then. After his remark about the welcome sign, Renee watched to see if his full attention was on the street as they drove. It took heart to appreciate a place like Dry Creek. The man's focus never wavered, though. Finally, she decided he missed the place. For some reason, that gave her a good deal of satisfaction. Maybe he wasn't as bad as that cat-loving gangster after all.

"The nativity practice is at the old Elkton barn on the other side of town," Renee said. "I don't know if you remember the place."

He nodded. "No one was using it when I was a boy, but I'd go inside sometimes to admire the construction of the loft."

She looked at him. "I heard it was the old make-out place for the high school kids. Before it was given to the town, of course."

"Maybe, but I went for the architecture," he answered smoothly. "Even back then, no one was making barns like that."

He didn't manage to look her in the eye, but she let it go.

When she turned, Renee saw the snow-covered barn come into view on the left side of the road. The pastor's wife, Glory Curtis, had spearheaded an effort to paint a historical mural on the structure some years ago and it was spectacular, with its wheat fields and pioneers in wagons.

"They do the nativity pageant there every year now so they can use real animals," Renee said, feeling pride even though it had started before she lived in the area.

"Like the donkey Eric claims to have," Rusty said.

"And sheep," Renee added. "The shepherd boys use their dogs for practice, but on the night of the performance there will be a few sheep."

"I could bring Dog."

"He'd scare the shepherds. The angels, too."

Rusty shrugged. "So everyone will be at the practice?"

"Eric and Karyn should be there, if that's what you

want to know." Renee answered his unspoken question. "Although the younger kids will be the main focus."

"Like Tessie?"

Renee nodded. "Mrs. Hargrove will bring her."

Then she continued, "Remember, you can't act like a prince when you talk to Tessie. Don't be too nice. You're supposed to convince her you don't have any fairy-tale qualities."

"I expect she'll see that right away."

Renee didn't say anything. She hoped her daughter was smart enough to understand this man wasn't a prince. If she could manage that one small thing, it would be the first step in getting a better picture of her father.

Renee parked in front of the barn and turned around to pull a large bag of bathrobes out of the backseat. She was in charge of the costumes, and the pageant workers had traditionally relied on local people to donate their used clothing. Some women bought new white cotton robes each fall just so they could give their old ones to the angels. The men generally bought brown or gray robes, so a simple cord could turn the boys into rough shepherds.

By the time Renee faced her door, she saw that Rusty was already standing there with his left hand on the outside door handle, waiting to help her exit the vehicle.

"At your service, m'lady," he said as he opened the door and offered his hand.

She scowled at him. "I don't think a prince says *m'lady*. He'd be above titles."

"I just didn't want *you* to think I couldn't be a polite prince if need be," he said, his voice soft and intimate.

"Very funny." She let him carry the bag of robes into the barn.

Guilt overcame her by the time they stepped inside and she insisted on being the one to take everything over to where Mrs. Hargrove stood. The man should not be carrying things around with one arm in a sling, she told herself.

Besides, she admitted, she didn't want to start any rumors about herself and the strange man who'd been shot last night. She knew that story would have gone all around town by now, so she and Rusty couldn't afford to look as if they were together.

In her quest to show indifference, Renee decided to ignore Rusty as she walked over to a few bales of hay where Mrs. Hargrove was sitting and started talking to her. The older woman had very definite opinions about which robes should go with which roles in the pageant and Renee was grateful for every one of her suggestions. Then the woman picked up a large silk bathrobe in a deep purple.

"That's perfect for King Herod, if we can ever find a man willing to play the part," Mrs. Hargrove said. "I know someone donates a fancy bathrobe every year just to keep us guessing who it is, but this time they brought the right thing. I can just see our Herod standing in this and trying to trick the wise men."

There was a black lace inset in the back of the robe and the sleeves were gathered into a bell shape of some kind. Black velvet piping was sewn onto the collar.

"I think it's a woman's robe," Renee said cautiously.

"It might be easier to find a guy to play the part if he doesn't have to wear this."

"Well, we can't have the king up on stage in his overalls," Mrs. Hargrove said firmly. "There's no reason this couldn't be a king's robe anyway. Nobility liked fancy clothes like that two thousand years ago. Remember, men were the first ones to wear high heels."

"I suppose," Renee agreed reluctantly. Besides, since they weren't getting any males willing to play the part, King Herod would likely end up being played by a tall woman anyway. There must have been a Queen Herod. Renee finished emptying the bag of robes before she realized that Rusty was nowhere to be seen. She had left him standing by the doorway, beside the row of hooks that had been added for coats. She supposed he had gone looking for his brother.

"What about this green robe?" Mrs. Hargrove fingered one of the donations. "Do you think it would work for Joseph?"

The robe had no decorations and the color was as close to brown as it was to green. It looked like that army color, in fact.

"Why, yes, I do believe it would be perfect," Renee said. Even a teenager like Eric Calhoun could not object to that costume.

By that time, the older woman was looking at yet another robe and Renee forgot about everything else.

Rusty had recognized Mrs. Hargrove the minute he stepped into the barn, even with all of the shadows. He hadn't wanted her to see him, though.

He remembered the woman well. She'd invited him

and his brother to Sunday school several times, but his father hadn't thought it was important and they hadn't gone. He'd watched her from a distance back in those days and wondered what it would be like to have a mother like her. But he hadn't known her, not really.

He'd been flat-out surprised when he got a card from her a few months after he joined the army. She had written a few things about Dry Creek, mostly how the crops were doing and how winter was expected early that year, and he thought that would be the end of it.

But it wasn't. She'd sent him dozens of cards and letters in the past eight years. Square blue envelopes. Long yellow ones. Even a box of homemade fudge one Christmas. She told him about the new gas station in town and what Pastor Curtis was preaching. She filled him in on her marriage to her old friend Charlie and listed all the babies who were born. The cards and letters were all different, but each was signed "Praying for you, Edith Hargrove."

Except for postcards from Eric now and then, they were the only mail he received. Rusty kept them through the years, gathered together with a thick rubber band in his duffel. He never answered the letters, though. It was as if he was tongue-tied and didn't know what to say. A woman like her didn't need the details of the misery he went through on patrols, and he had nothing else to talk about. With each letter he received, he expected it to be the last. But it never was.

And now here she was, looking just the same as he remembered her, with her gray hair tucked back in those tight permanent waves and her green-and-white-checked housedress hanging loose under her gray wool sweater. If he remembered right, the kids said she always had some kind of wrapped candy in her pocket for any child who wanted a piece. He'd never had the nerve to ask for one the few times he was around her.

He was glad she hadn't seen him come in behind Renee. He had turned in the opposite direction and walked. He still didn't know what to say to someone like her. The only mother he'd known had been his own and she'd never seemed to notice him much. He didn't expect someone else's mother to take to him. Not that he needed a mother anyway.

Still, he hadn't been in this old barn for years and he enjoyed the chance to see it. The air smelled the same, of the mustiness that came from decades of stored alfalfa hay. The main walls were as tall as he remembered—he'd guess twenty feet high in all. Thankfully, no one had ever painted the inside of the barn, although they had added sealant over the years, so the walls had a natural wood sheen. He noticed with approval that the small, high windows lining each side of the barn were sparkling clean. Someone was taking good care of this place.

Rusty was walking by a piece of the nativity setting when he heard a whimper. He turned and frowned. The no-vacancy sign was hanging from a fake inn door and a false front was painted to look like beige stone. No one was behind the plywood, so he stood and listened.

There he heard it again, deeper, from the corner of the barn. It sounded like a muffled sob. Suddenly, he heard several mocking voices that seemed to be coming from behind a set of portable bleachers. He carefully picked his way toward the noise.

The children didn't hear him as he looked around the edge of the bleachers. They were all in the shadows and no one was facing his direction. A blanket had been tacked over the barn window in this corner and the children seemed to be waiting there. Except they weren't really waiting. At first, he wondered if they had a dice game going since they were all gathered in a circle and looking at something intently.

The hay bales in the corner were spread around and several of the boys were sitting on them.

Then he saw Tessie. She was sitting in the middle of the circle on the rough wood floor and the expression on her face made his heart clench. She was trying bravely not to cry, but her bottom lip was trembling. Her face was pink.

"That's what you know, Mikey Lane," she finally said and pointed accusingly at one of the bigger boys. "He is so real."

The boy, who was standing before her, snorted in disgust. "You're such a baby. Nobody believes in fairy tales."

Rusty must have moved then, because Tessie looked over Mikey's head and saw him. Her face lit up as though she'd seen every one of her dreams come true. Then she scrambled to her feet and pointed again. Only this time it was at him.

"There he is!" she declared victoriously. "The prince who has come to see me."

Rusty just stood there, feeling like a bug pinned to a specimen board. He was hoping no one would turn to look, but of course, they all did. He was glad he'd shaved this morning. He stood up straight, but there was no fooling the boys.

Each one of them stared in disbelief. He glared back. It was obvious that no one but little Tessie thought he was a prince, but he didn't like the boys making fun of her. Faith should be rewarded even if it was misplaced.

"You're not a prince," Mikey, obviously the leader of this little band of troublemakers, said with enough disgust in his voice to make Rusty arch his eyebrow.

"He is so." Tessie stood and then did the most remarkable thing. She ran toward him as fast as she could. She was fleeing her enemies, with her white angel robe flapping and her wings wobbling behind her.

When she reached Rusty, she held out her arms.

"Up," she commanded.

Rusty closed his eyes and wondered if Renee would ever forgive him.

If he hadn't seen the tears in Tessie's eyes, he might have had the courage to remain still. But he could see that while she might be angry with those boys, she was scared, too.

He had no choice but to bend down. He grimaced as he put his good arm around her, but he lifted her anyway. Maybe he shouldn't have done that, he thought as her wings fluttered when he drew her close. She didn't disturb his sling, but he could feel the weight of her, especially with those wings moving around.

The pain wasn't anything bad, but Tessie opened her eyes and put her hand up to his face. She looked worried about him. Just the way her mother always seemed to be.

"It's okay," he said softly and she settled against the left side of his chest, leaving his sling untouched.

After she drew a few ragged breaths, he felt her relax in his arms. He'd never had a child snuggle into him before and he found it rather alarming. He wasn't sure he knew what to do with the trust of someone like Tessie. He left that to men who'd known a regular family life. Just thinking about it almost made him forget to keep an eye on the boys.

He looked up to see the troublemakers still gawking at Tessie, disgust on their faces, so he did the only thing he could: he scowled and gave them his mean look. The one that had made green recruits tremble in their boots and wish they were home with their mothers. Then he added a snarl because boys that age needed something extra to understand the message.

He was rewarded with faces of astonishment. One of the youngest boys turned as if he might run for the door, but they all looked respectful. Rusty decided his work was done, but then he realized something. That look of awe was going on for too long and no one had fled the area.

"He's the one," Mikey finally announced as he lifted one arm to give a victory salute. Then he turned to the other boys. "Did you see that face? Oh, yeah, he's the one."

"Who's going to tell Mrs. Hargrove?" one of the other boys asked, already fidgeting in his eagerness to be off.

That was all it took. They ran away as fast as they could.

Rusty just watched them go.

He'd certainly slain Tessie's dragons just the way a good prince should. But he wasn't quite sure what to do next. He almost felt as if he should take on defending Tessie on a regular basis, and that would never do. Especially not when Renee had told him to break the little girl's heart. He wasn't meant to be the hero in her story.

But the least he could do was carry the girl away with dignity, he told himself. Her mother would know what to do with Tessie next.

Once he stepped around the bleachers, he saw Renee on the other side of the barn standing by some hay bales with Mrs. Hargrove. A dozen robes lay over the top of those bales, but the women weren't even looking at them. They were intent on the boys who were standing in front of them and gesturing all over the place.

Rusty figured that he could just drop Tessie off near her mother and sneak out of the barn in all the commotion.

He didn't even get close before he saw it wasn't going to happen.

Mikey was already pointing at him. By now, he assumed the boys had told Mrs. Hargrove how mean he'd been to them. He'd forgotten how boys could be. But it was probably for the best. He wouldn't have to worry about Tessie wanting him to stay and be her prince once she heard the tales that were sure to come.

Rusty kept walking. His exit might not be so quiet, but it would be quick.

He was surprised when Mrs. Hargrove started walking toward him. "Rusty Calhoun, is that you?"

"Yes, ma'am." He acknowledged his name, although he wasn't sure why she would recognize him after all

this time. He'd been a skinny kid when he left Dry
Creek. He was considerably taller now. And he liked
to think he was better-looking if for no other reason
than that the military had taught him not to slouch.

The boys didn't hold back. He saw them following
along behind the older woman as though they didn't
want to miss any part of this show.

Rusty sent an imploring look to Renee. She was
standing in a stream of sunlight coming through a back
window that made her brown hair look as if it had been
spun with a bit of gold. They'd almost been in an accident together. He just knew she was going to stand up
for him—and then she shrugged.

Mrs. Hargrove stopped and looked at him for a minute.

He'd been wrong about her, too, he decided when
she was close. She had changed since he'd seen her last:
wrinkles crisscrossed her face where there had been
none before. Her eyes looked tired. He really should
have answered her letters, he told himself.

Then she opened her arms to him.

He didn't even think as he slid Tessie down to the
floor and gathered the older woman in a one-armed
embrace.

"You came back to us," Mrs. Hargrove said as she
hugged him tight. "Praise God." She pulled back then.
"Let me look at you."

Rusty grinned. He had come home and he hadn't
known it until that very moment.

"My prayers have been answered," Mrs. Hargrove
said, her face beaming.

Rusty heard one of the boys clear his throat. Then

another one did. Finally Mrs. Hargrove looked down at the fidgeting boys.

"That's what we were trying to tell you," Mikey announced. "Your prayers have been answered. We found you King Herod."

Mikey took a deep breath and made a dramatic gesture with his arm. "Him."

Mrs. Hargrove looked as stunned by the proclamation as Rusty felt. He glanced over at Renee again—she seemed speechless.

"You won't have to worry about getting him to make a mean face," Mikey said confidently. "He does a real good one. Sound effects and everything."

"I couldn't possibly—" Rusty said as he took a step backward.

"Why not?" Mrs. Hargrove pinned Rusty with a hopeful glance. "You're the one person in Dry Creek who has never played a part in the pageant. It's time we fixed that."

"I'm not much for pageants," Rusty said, taking another step backward.

"Renee can help you learn your lines," Mrs. Hargrove said.

Now Renee took some action. "He can't be in the pageant!" she protested vigorously. She shook her head as though searching for something more to say. Finally, she stammered, "He is wounded."

That didn't seem to get a response so she added, "And he could be a criminal."

Rusty hated to be rescued with those words, but he decided he wouldn't defend himself. It was better to have people cross the street when they saw him than it would be to appear in the pageant.

But Mrs. Hargrove only nodded thoughtfully. "Oh, I'm sure he hasn't broken any laws. And if he looks a little dangerous, that makes him a good King Herod, who was an old crook if there ever was one."

With that, Tessie spoke. She was short and her voice was low, but everyone heard her. "He's a prince, so he can play the king real good."

Mrs. Hargrove beamed.

Renee scowled.

And Rusty squatted down to speak with the girl. "Sometimes things are make-believe—"

That was as far as he got before Mrs. Hargrove cleared her throat.

Rusty looked up and saw Sheriff Wall standing not three feet away. Maybe it was because he was down on Tessie's level, but the sheriff looked particularly stern and foreboding.

Rusty rose to his feet.

The sheriff pulled a plastic evidence bag out of his coat and unzipped it.

"Ever see this before?" he asked as he held out Eric's old brown cap.

Rusty resisted the urge to look around. He hadn't seen his brother as he walked around the barn. He surely couldn't be here.

"I don't know," Rusty said truthfully enough. It might or might not be the cap he'd seen last night.

"I found it in that ravine you mentioned," the sheriff said then. "Looks like one of those caps your brother always wears."

"I haven't been around this area for eight years," Rusty reminded the sheriff.

Sheriff Wall measured him. "That's so. Makes me wonder what you're doing back here now."

Rusty bit back a reply.

"Why, God brought him here to play King Herod," Mrs. Hargrove said in a voice that was mixed with steel and kindness. She stepped forward and put her hand on Rusty's left arm. "And we're very glad to have him."

That set the sheriff back. He turned to Rusty. "You're playing the king?"

Rusty nodded reluctantly.

"Well, then," the sheriff said as he put the cap back in the bag, "I'll leave you all to what you're doing. I'll have the whole church mad at me if I chase off a king now that we found one."

The lawman put the bag back inside his jacket as he checked everyone out. If the moment hadn't been so silent, Rusty would have remarked that the sheriff had a downright mean look, too, and could play King Herod as well as anyone else.

"Tell Eric I'd like to talk to him," Sheriff Wall finally said to Rusty as he turned to leave. "Since I can't believe he'd take a shot at his own brother, he might want to take a look at the kind of company he is keeping."

Rusty was of the same opinion, so he gave the sheriff an agreeable nod.

The sheriff looked around again, this time peering into the corners of the barn. "Shouldn't the boy be here? I heard he's Joseph in this pageant."

"Mary's not here, either," Mrs. Hargrove offered,

and then she turned to Renee. "Karyn's not taking the noon shift for you at the bunkhouse, is she?"

Renee shook her head. "I left a pot roast cooking for the men. The table's all set and a salad tucked in the refrigerator. She should be here practicing."

Sheriff Wall looked thoughtful. "The two of them kids might still be out at the Elkton ranch. Not many places to wander to on a cold day like this." He turned to Renee. "Mind if I drive out and check?"

"Not at all," Renee said with a smile. "If you follow us out, we'll all be in time for pot roast. I might even pull one of those cherry pies that you like so much out of the freezer."

Rusty didn't see why she needed to make it so inviting. He would rather have a chance to sit down with his brother and talk privately before the law got involved. Of course, he could hardly say anything without making the sheriff more determined to go with them.

"Now, that'd be nice," Sheriff Wall said.

"You don't mind if Tessie and I take King Herod and leave?" Renee asked Mrs. Hargrove.

The older woman shook her head. "You go right ahead. That might be best. The rest of us will practice. We'll fit King Herod with his costume at tomorrow's practice. Only four more nights until the performance, you know. And there's church tomorrow." Mrs. Hargrove looked directly at Rusty. "I'm hoping we'll see you in services tomorrow."

Rusty was going to decline, but then she said, "I wasn't the only one to pray for you. I might have been the only one to write, but the whole church prayed for you."

Rusty was still trying to find a way to say he wasn't coming.

"I would consider it a personal favor if you came," Mrs. Hargrove said, a soft light in her eyes.

Rusty hadn't been looked at with love many times in his life, but he recognized it all the same. Even his own mother had never written him a letter.

His voice was thick. "I'll be there."

"Good." Mrs. Hargrove smiled at him.

Rusty gathered up Tessie and escaped to the pickup before any of the boys could see King Herod with damp eyes. He figured Renee wouldn't be too pleased about him going to church, since he'd have to get a ride with her. He'd be sure to sit in a separate pew, as touchy as she was about anyone thinking they might know each other.

Not that he wanted any gossip to start, either, he told himself. Renee was a delicate butterfly of a woman— flitting here and there. Always beautiful, but with a wonderful array of emotions he'd never figure out.

She was the kind of woman lost to him, he told himself. His mother had been that way from the first, he remembered. Sparkling with emotion until life with his father had pulled the joy right out of her. Rusty was cut out of the same taciturn cloth as all the Calhoun men. He could not bear for the coldness inside of him to take away the joy inside of Renee. Some things in life were just worse than being alone.

Chapter Four

Renee stomped across the snow to the driver's door of the pickup and then frowned. A few snowflakes were still falling and the air was icy cold. It was going to be a white Christmas, but that didn't bring her much cheer at the moment.

"She needs to ride in the booster seat," she informed the prince flatly as she climbed inside. "And you don't have to carry her. She's five years old now and can walk on her own two feet. Besides, you have an arm in a sling."

She didn't know why he insisted on ignoring his injuries. By tomorrow he'd be in pain and, like as not, expect someone else to run around and fetch for him. Well, it wasn't going to be her.

"I know you're upset," Rusty said as he turned slightly so he could unlatch his door. "But it's no trouble. I can put her back where she needs to be easy enough."

Renee shook her head. But some of the anger had drained out of her. Tessie was asleep and Rusty first had to remove the girl's cardboard wings and set them on the floor. He did that very carefully, then started to strap Tessie into her seat. Since he could use only his left arm, Renee had no choice but to step out of the cab and open the back door.

"Here, let me," she said as she climbed up into the backseat to get a proper angle on the seat belts. She pushed the seat closer to the opposite door and grabbed a pillow so that Tessie could rest her head and continue sleeping if she wanted. Last night had been late for them all and Tessie had woken up early this morning, still excited about her prince. Apparently Rusty had kept both her and her daughter awake last night. But it wasn't his fault he'd gotten to her.

Renee locked all the seat belts into place and scooted out of the back of the cab. Rusty had already settled himself in the passenger seat again. By the time Renee was back at the steering wheel, she was freezing and thoroughly discouraged.

She had no reason to care about this man. Just because he'd landed on her doorstep didn't mean she needed to worry about what would happen to him.

She turned on the ignition and hit the defrost button. That would give the cab some heat while it cleared the fog on the window. Fortunately, they had been away from the pickup only long enough for a layer of frost to form.

"I'm sorry things didn't go well in there," Rusty finally said after they had sat together in silence for what seemed like a very long time to Renee.

She turned to look at him. "I know you didn't intend to end up as King Herod."

The heater had cleared a small semicircle low on

the windshield. They still had a few minutes before it would grow enough for them to leave.

Rusty shrugged. "I didn't intend to rescue Tessie, either. I had every intention of proving I was no prince, but…" His voice trailed off. "Well, I couldn't just leave her there crying all by herself."

"I know," Renee said softly. "It's probably my fault anyway."

He looked up curiously. "How do you figure that?"

Renee told herself she shouldn't have started this discussion, but he might as well hear it from her before someone else told him. "People around here think I should be giving Tessie someone who can be a father figure to her so she doesn't invent imaginary princes. I mean, she has uncles and all, but she doesn't know them well, and—"

Renee stopped. It was none of his business why she didn't have a man in her life.

It was silent for so long that she didn't know whether to just put the vehicle in gear and back up or sit and wait for him to say something.

"You mean people want you to get married," he finally said, sounding puzzled, "just to have a father for Tessie?"

Put like that, it didn't seem like such a good idea.

"Well, I'm sure they want me to like the guy, too."

"And what do you do when you wake up someday and realize you are unhappy?" he challenged with a bit of anger in his voice. "That's not going to do your child any favors."

"I would never leave," Renee protested. Even in all of those awful days with her ex-husband, she had never left. Not even when she should have done so. Not even when he was arrested. She suddenly realized that maybe her ex-husband sending those divorce papers was an act of kindness and not something meant to upset her. Maybe he knew she could never bring herself to do it.

"I just never would," she finally said softly, her indignation spent.

Rusty was silent and they sat a few minutes more, even though the windshield had defrosted enough.

"My mother left," he said quietly. "It was a spring day. Her birthday. I gave her the pearl necklace I bought with my wages from Mr. Elkton. I was so proud. I just knew it would make her happy."

Renee reached over and touched his arm. "I'm sorry."

"I've done fine without her," Rusty said, his voice gaining strength. "I just don't want you to make the same mistake. Who do people think you should marry anyway?"

"Barry Grover." Renee turned her attention back to the wheel.

She wasn't so sure Rusty should be confiding in her or she in him. She knew sometimes strangers told each other things that they didn't tell those close to them, but it made her uneasy. Still, since he'd told her something so personal, she owed him.

"So what's so special about Barry?" Rusty was looking at her, his brown eyes serious.

Renee shifted the vehicle into Reverse and started to back up. "They say he's steady. And I want that."

"Steady?" Rusty sounded bewildered.

Renee nodded. "Regular job. No call to adventure. You know, the kind of man who can give me and Tessie our own house. Not that I mind living in the cook's quarters at the ranch, but there's not much room. Not even space for a desk for Tessie when she starts having homework. Or a bedroom for her when she's older. I sleep on the sofa and she sleeps on a small cot."

Rusty nodded.

"And he can make my later years golden," she added in all fairness to Barry.

Renee checked in the rearview mirror to be sure Tessie was sleeping.

"Really? Stocks? Property?" Rusty asked.

"Pension," Renee said as she turned the pickup around and started on the road home to the Elkton ranch. "From the postal service."

"Oh," Rusty murmured. "I suppose that's important."

She could tell he meant no such thing and she couldn't say anything, because she agreed with him. She might marry for security, but it wasn't financial security. She wanted a home, but it could be small. She didn't care if her husband was a mailman or the president of the United States. She wanted someone who would care about her and Tessie.

The roads were clear and the pickup ran smoothly. Renee noticed that some of the shrubs were white with ice. The barbed-wire fences stretched out on both sides of the gravel road. The sky was gray and came down to meet the barren ground around them like a bowl set over the earth.

She looked in the rearview mirror and assured herself that the sheriff was following in his patrol car.

"Maybe we can work on the not-being-a-prince thing tomorrow," she finally said. "Tessie had a hard time today. Tomorrow is soon enough to crush her hopes."

Rusty turned to stare at her.

"Is that what will happen if I tell her I'm not her prince?" he protested in horror. "I figured she'd be a little unsettled, but I don't want to upset her that much."

Renee looked over. The man had actually turned pale. "I don't see how you have a choice. What she really wants is the message you're supposed to have from her father. Do you have one?"

"Of course not," Rusty said, his color coming back. "But there's not much I can do about that."

"Well, there you have it," she said.

Before long, they were turning onto the Elkton ranch property. Renee always liked the large wooden sign hanging between two massive logs that towered over the road leading into the place. The ranch hands maintained the road, clearing snow in the winter and fixing potholes in the summer.

"My father always said this sign was a waste of good trees," Rusty said with a slight smile. "My mother loved it, though. Claimed it was the sign of a civilized ranch, where people stopped for tea in the afternoon and understood the art of conversation."

Renee shrugged. "They mostly drink coffee in the bunkhouse."

"I suppose so."

"But I love the sign, too," Renee added.

Rusty nodded.

Ordinarily, she'd go to the cook's quarters, but since Tessie's things were in the main house, she planned to stop there first and get some toys before she drove all three of them over to the bunkhouse to eat pot roast. Tessie should change her clothes, too.

"Can I help with anything?" Rusty asked when she stopped the pickup in front of the Elkton house porch. He unbuckled his seat belt and turned around to look at Tessie. "Should I carry her inside?"

"Not with your shoulder," Renee said.

"It's okay," he said as he opened his door. "She's not that heavy."

"You'll pay the price tomorrow," Renee said, but she nodded.

It suddenly occurred to her that Tessie might react differently to the man when she wasn't desperate for rescue. Her daughter didn't trust easily. Maybe it would be worthwhile to see how she greeted her prince now.

"Tessie," Rusty whispered as he stood outside the back door of the cab and undid the seat belts holding the girl upright. "I'm going to carry you inside, so if you can just wake up a little bit, I can do that."

"Kiss me," her daughter said drowsily.

"What?" Rusty straightened up and looked at Renee in almost comical panic.

Renee hid her smile. "Sleeping Beauty. She likes to play that with me. The prince needs to kiss the princess to make her wake up."

She whispered to Rusty, "A pretend kiss will do."

The mischief returned to Rusty's eyes and he leaned back over Tessie. "Now, I wonder, what happens if the prince doesn't kiss the princess? Does she turn into a spider?"

With that, Rusty walked his fingers up Tessie's arm until he got to her neck.

By that time Tessie was giggling so hard she opened her eyes and squealed in delight.

All of them quieted down when the sheriff's car pulled in beside them. Renee decided Tessie didn't need a toy. Not when she had her prince to amuse her.

"We can just go over to the bunkhouse," Renee said. "The pot roast should be done by now."

The air in the pickup didn't even have a chance to cool off in the minute it took to drive past the barn and corrals and come to the front of the bunkhouse. Renee watched without comment as Tessie lifted her arms out to Rusty and he gathered her up to carry her inside.

Rusty didn't know what he expected in a place where bachelor cowboys lived, but it wasn't this. Renee had opened the door to a room rich with green plants and wood flooring. The diamond-paned windows were covered with white gauze curtains. Three overstuffed brown leather couches were gathered to one side around a fireplace made of river rock. A round oak table that looked as if it would seat fifteen people stood in the middle of the room. Two decks of cards sat on the table ready to use. He picked one of them up and saw it had a picture of clouds and a Western couple on it that advertised some book. *The ranch hands must read.* Tessie held her hand out for the cards, but he put the deck down on the coffee table.

"They are not ours," he whispered in the girl's ear.

"Pretty," she said.

He nodded and looked down the long hallway to his right. The hall went straight and he counted four doors on each side.

He always thought that men who lived alone did so with clutter and an absence of light and pleasing color. There had certainly been no softness to his family's ranch house after his mother left. But this bunkhouse could be on the cover of one of those gracious-living magazines. He wondered if it was Renee's doing.

"You're lucky to have your mama," Rusty whispered in Tessie's ear as he set her on one of the couches. He was almost certain Renee could hang curtains in a cave if that was where she lived.

Little Tessie looked up at him solemnly and nodded.

The sheriff had followed them in the door, but he had sat down and was using the bunkhouse phone. He'd said he couldn't get cell reception and had to return some calls.

Rusty went over to the tall Christmas tree that stood in the corner of the room. It was decorated with old horseshoes and white coiled rope. Even a few silver spurs were added on the thicker branches. Pine cones were tied here and there with red ribbons.

"That's some tree," he said and turned around to search for Renee.

"Give me a hand," she said from where she stood in front of an old-fashioned walnut buffet. The doors were open and she was pulling out a stack of cast-iron trivets. "I should have put these on the table when I set the plates earlier. That way I can leave the pot roast in the pans."

Rusty stepped over and reached with his good arm. Renee hesitated and finally gave him four of the trivets. "I forgot about your shoulder. You need to rest your arms. It can't be doing you any good to move either one of them so much."

No one had fussed over him since—he stopped a moment to try to remember. No one had ever bothered with how he felt, except for Mrs. Hargrove and now Renee. That was two people in one day. He wondered if the planets were still in alignment or if the whole universe was in as much shock as he was.

"My shoulder is fine," he said as he carried the trivets to the table.

Rusty made another trip for napkins and helped Renee place them on the left side of each of the twelve plates. He found he kind of liked doing a domestic chore like this with her. Eight years in the army had accustomed him to tin plates and plastic forks. Renee used heavy white stoneware and good quality silver-plated utensils. He didn't need to be told these meals were important to her and that people often lingered afterward for conversation.

Some women just naturally knew how to build a home—a family, really—and he suspected Renee was one of them.

Sheriff Wall was just finishing his calls when Rusty heard a faint sound of something outside. He looked at the plank door and saw it was securely closed. Not locked, but not moving in the wind. The windows looked out into the snowy yard of the Elkton ranch. No cattle were loose; no dogs barking. He planned to look up Dog after dinner, but the sounds weren't coming from him. Rusty strained to hear and the sound came closer. It was low-pitched giggling.

"Can you keep an eye on Tessie?" Renee said as she turned to him. "I'll run over to the cook's house and get the pot roast."

Those giggles were charged with more than good cheer.

"Wait a minute," Rusty said as he put up his hand for silence. Some of the tones sounded familiar. And he heard the soft tread of a boot on the boardwalk outside the door.

He took a step forward to prevent what he now knew was likely to happen, but it was too late.

In a burst of snowflakes, denim jeans and swirling long brown hair, his brother, Eric, and another teenager stumbled through the doorway and into the bunkhouse. If it hadn't been for the laughter still bubbling up from Eric, Rusty would not have known him. He'd talked to his brother almost every week since he'd left Dry Creek, but he hadn't seen him. A few school pictures were all he had to measure the boy.

His brother had shot up from five and a half feet to what must be a full six feet two inches tall. He was skinny, though, and had the same Calhoun slouch Rusty had at his age. Fortunately, the long hair belonged to the girl and not his brother. Rusty couldn't say much about his brother's posture, but he just might say something about the tattoo of a dragon that curled around the boy's forearm, half of it covered by the sleeve of a white T-shirt.

It was Eric's eyes that surprised Rusty most. They

were lit up with something he'd never seen on his brother's face before—pure joy.

He had his arm looped around the neck of the petite young woman who was smiling up at Eric with as much delight as he seemed to have looking down at her.

And then Eric's eyes adjusted to the inside light.

"What are you doing here?" He stared at Rusty in confusion.

Rusty didn't answer and tried to make eye contact with his brother to urge him to keep silent. Sometimes, the less said, the better. He noticed his brother wasn't wearing a cap, but Rusty could still see the mark the band had made on Eric's forehead.

"Surprised to see your older brother, are you?" Sheriff Wall said as he stepped farther into the room. He'd hung up the phone and had no doubt seen it all.

No one said anything as the sheriff faced the two young people. The lawman scanned both Eric and the girl before focusing on the first of them.

"Where were you last night?" the sheriff asked Eric, bringing all the power of his badge to the question.

"He was with me." The girl leaped into the silence before Eric could answer. She took a step forward, almost as though she was shielding him from the lawman.

"Karyn," Renee said softly as she stepped closer to the young woman and put a hand on her arm. "The sheriff is only asking."

Rusty was pleased to note that Eric did not hide behind his girlfriend, but stepped to the side and then closer so that the shield was reversed. Eric put an arm around Karyn and stared defiantly at the sheriff.

Rusty noted his brother didn't answer the question and was staring at him.

"What happened to you?" Eric asked Rusty. "Run into trouble?"

"He was shot last night," the sheriff said, his voice slicing through any small talk anyone was thinking of making. "At that ravine where you lost your cap."

Rusty knew the sheriff was bluffing on that last bit, but he didn't know how to warn his brother.

Eric's face had already gone white. No glimmer of joy remained.

"You were there?" he asked quietly, looking at Rusty in concern.

Rusty bit back a groan.

"Who else was there?" the sheriff asked, pressing his advantage.

Eric shrugged. "I can't tell you that. Not yet, anyway."

"You can tell the lawman," Rusty said, hoping his brother would listen to reason. It wouldn't do Eric any good to protect the man in the orange parka.

Eric just shook his head. "We weren't doing anything."

Rusty knew better than that, but he didn't want to talk to his brother in front of the sheriff. He could see the other man already knew something was wrong with Eric's answers.

Everyone was silent for a few minutes.

Then the girl, Karyn, hiccuped.

"What's wrong?" she wailed and twined herself around Eric.

Eric's face turned red as he tried to curl himself

around the girl, likely so the sheriff couldn't see her or hear what she was mumbling about.

The lawman didn't seem inclined to listen to Karyn anyway, not when he could stare down his nose at Rusty.

"What?" Rusty finally protested.

"I'm hoping you have sense enough to tell me what you and your brother are involved in," Sheriff Wall said to Rusty, his voice dead serious. "This morning I figured you were just in the wrong place at the wrong time. Now I'm beginning to think that maybe you're bringing the trouble with you."

"I haven't done anything," Rusty said.

"Then why'd you end up with that bullet in you?" The lawman shot back the question. "Did your brother have anything to do with it?"

"I think we need an attorney," Rusty finally said.

The sheriff was silent for a minute.

"If that's the way you want to play it, I can put you in touch with a lawyer," the lawman said. "You're not being arrested. I am asking you to stay in the area, though."

The sheriff gave each of them a thorough study—Rusty, Eric and then Karyn. "I'm holding each of you responsible for the other two. Any one of you leaves, you're all in trouble."

Karyn hiccuped again.

Rusty stepped over to the sheriff and whispered, "Look, leave the girl out of it. She didn't have anything to do with what happened."

Sheriff Wall looked up at him. "Yeah, but she'll keep your brother around. That's enough."

Rusty looked over to see Eric patting his girlfriend on the back. Then he glanced over at Renee and wished he hadn't. She was staring at him as if she held him responsible for every tear that poor girl was shedding.

"I didn't do anything," he said to her.

"Oh, you men" was all she said as she walked over to rub Karyn's back.

Rusty thought this would likely mean that the invitation to eat would be snatched away. But just then the ranch hands started coming in from the corrals and barn. They stomped into the room, their loud voices drowning out the girl's sobbing.

"We could smell pot roast when we were halfway here," one man said as he pulled a straight-backed chair out from the table. He looked over at Rusty. "That wolf dog of yours smelled it, too. I think he's staying right outside the window there—hoping for a handout. Better give it to him. I wouldn't want to rile him if I were you."

The man pointed to a window that was open a couple of inches. "Fresh air."

"Dog is friendly," Rusty told the men. "Just takes him a bit to get to know you."

"You're saying he's shy?" the ranch hand protested in astonishment. "He's half the size of that horse of yours—and she's so pregnant she's almost ready to deliver. I'll eat my hat if that wolf dog of yours is shy."

"Well, he's had a hard time these past few years," Rusty insisted. "He'll need to get used to you."

It was silent for a minute as the ranch hands absorbed his words and then nodded. They'd likely had some rough patches in their lives, too. And they likely knew that looking tough on the outside didn't mean the pain went away any faster on the inside.

"I hope you put lots of carrots in with the beef," another man said then, turning to Renee.

She nodded.

Rusty suspected Renee didn't quite know what to do, but she finally just excused herself to go to the cook's kitchen to get the pot roast. Karyn pulled herself together and followed Renee, saying she was going to help.

Eric and Rusty were left to stare at each other. It was a slow thaw, but Eric's lips gradually turned up into a smile and Rusty grinned back.

"I'm glad you're here," Eric said.

Rusty walked over and thumped his brother on the back. "You never even told me you had a girlfriend."

"Well…" Eric blushed, but didn't say any more.

"Yeah, well," Rusty agreed as he put his good arm around his brother's shoulders.

They just stood there together for a minute while the ranch hands all seemed to find a place at the table.

"I didn't mean to make Karyn cry," Eric finally said in a low voice. "It's just, I'll do something and she gets all upset and I don't even know what it was that set her off."

Rusty offered what sympathy he could. "We Calhouns don't know much about women."

"Ain't that the truth," Eric agreed.

Rusty had never thought he'd see his baby brother in love.

The sad truth was that they were right. Their father had often said the Calhoun men were hopeless when it came to women, and Rusty had always agreed. It had taken him some years in the military to realize his father could simply have been kinder to his mother. He didn't need to understand her to do that much.

"So Dog's with you?" Eric finally asked.

Rusty nodded. "I couldn't leave him at the Morgans' when I went riding last night. He wanted to come and when he saw I was bringing Annie, he practically begged."

It was only then that Rusty realized the two women were taking a long time to bring the food to the table. Which couldn't be good, he told himself as he looked over at the sheriff. The lawman was still glancing at him with suspicion, but all Rusty could do was smile back.

Chapter Five

Renee did all of her cooking for the ranch hands in the front half of the small cabin off the walkway in front of the bunkhouse. The cook's quarters were in the back part of the cabin. The walkway had an overhang to keep the snow and rain away as the food was brought to the table so that, even though some flakes were falling now, Renee and Karyn could have easily carried everything into the bunkhouse by now.

But they weren't ready to face all of the men yet.

Renee had pulled two large roasters, smelling of cooked beef and root vegetables, out of the oven and set them on the top of the gas stove. The scent of braised onions and garlic warmed the plain room. On the counter next to the pans, a large glass bowl held a huge mound of lettuce with diced fresh tomatoes, mushrooms and grated Parmesan cheese. A basket with two dozen wheat dinner rolls sat on the other side of the counter. Two cubes of butter were on a small crystal plate next to that.

"Here. Drink this. It'll get rid of those hiccups." Renee gave Karyn some water.

The girl did what she was told. Then she handed the empty glass back to Renee.

What little sun there was on this overcast day came through the room's side window and fell on the Karyn's face. It didn't seem to warm her, though.

"I lied," the girl confessed. Her face was blotchy and Renee thought she looked miserable. She was standing next to the door with her shoulders hunched and her feet restlessly tapping.

"Eric wasn't with me last night," she added finally and slowed her fidgeting. "I don't know where he was."

"I think we all figured that one out," Renee said, trying not to judge the girl too harshly. The poor thing was only seventeen. "But I hope you know you can get in all kinds of trouble by lying to the sheriff."

"I know," Karyn muttered with her head down and her voice small.

Renee debated whether to scold the girl some more, but decided she'd been scared enough.

"Do you think Eric did something bad?" Karyn asked, lifting her head. "Something illegal?"

Renee shrugged. "Both brothers might be doing something criminal."

She hadn't been expecting it, but Renee noticed her eyes were damp now, too. She told herself she shouldn't be surprised. She'd known all along that Rusty was likely up to no good out there last night.

"I suppose it is the rustling." She finally said the words they both dreaded.

Karyn swallowed. "Well, at least they aren't out killing people."

"Don't do that," Renee said more sharply than she intended.

"What?" Karyn looked bewildered.

"Try to make it better than it is," Renee said, all of her weariness coming out.

"Oh."

Renee faced the girl. "Rusty was shot last night. He would have died if he hadn't made his way to the Elktons' place. Somebody out there is shooting to kill. It wasn't an accident. Someone is doing something very wrong and Rusty must be involved in some way."

"I suppose," Karyn agreed.

They were silent for a while.

"Sorry I pressed you so hard," Renee apologized. "But I used to do that with my husband. I'd try to find a way to make his actions seem better so that I could live with them. It never worked. He got worse and worse and there I was with my head in the clouds and trouble happening all around me."

"Did you love him?" Karyn asked softly, all her own agony showing in her eyes. "Your husband?"

"I thought I did," Renee said and then added with a smile, "just like you probably think you love Eric."

Karyn was quiet, looking at the floor with her hair hanging down and hiding her face.

"It's not a crime to love," Renee said then. "We just need to be smart. My mistake in not seeing my husband clearly didn't just affect me. It also hurt Tessie. She suffers now because I ignored the signs that he was turning into a thief and a liar. The children always—"

Karyn looked up.

Renee drew in her breath with the sudden thought. "You're not—?"

Karyn shook her head vigorously. "No, we haven't even done anything. We wouldn't. But I want to have babies with Eric—someday when we're married. Now I wonder if he would be a good father."

Renee opened her arms to the girl.

"All I can say then is that you need to go slow," she told Karyn as she embraced her. "I believe Eric can turn his life around if he wants to—with God's help. I started a new life here in Dry Creek and I know anyone can."

Karyn stepped back from Renee's arms. She wiped her eyes and then nodded. "Yes, but how will I know if Eric and me—if we should be together?"

Renee looked at the girl. "Just ask some of the people in church. Mrs. Hargrove. My dad and his wife. The pastor. Ask Mr. and Mrs. Elkton when they get back."

Karyn's eyes went wide. "Ask everybody?"

Renee nodded. "Trust me—most of them already have an opinion on it. It might be good to hear what they all have to say."

"Wow," Karyn said, looking a little stunned.

"And don't forget to ask Betty Longe," Renee said. "She certainly knows all the names of eligible men around here. And she'll tell you what she thinks."

"Okay," Karyn said, squaring her shoulders. "Sort of like going to the elders for their advice? Like they did in the Bible."

"Exactly." Renee smiled at the girl and then turned to the counter. "Now, come help me. We have all those ranch hands to feed."

Renee walked across the small room to a counter and pulled out a cart from behind it that she often used. She rolled it up to the stove and they began to load the food on it. Tragedy might unfold and grief might surprise a person, but food seemed to be necessary in the midst of all of life's crises.

"Do you think they're still there?" Karyn asked as they pushed the cart out to the boardwalk.

Renee looked up, uncertain what Karyn was asking.

The boardwalk was damp from the fallen snow, but it wasn't slick. The metal wheels rumbled along the wooden planks well enough.

"Eric and his brother," Karyn clarified. "Do you think they could have gone away? Eric doesn't like hanging around lawmen."

"I don't know," Renee managed to say as they pushed the cart even faster.

The thought of Rusty not being there was upsetting to her, although she told herself her concerns were for Tessie. He was supposed to be watching Tessie, and even with all of the other adults there, Renee didn't like the thought that he might have just walked off and left her daughter without telling her. Then she saw Dog come around the corner. "They're here, all right."

"What's that thing?" Karyn asked, moving closer to Renee.

"Rusty calls him a dog, but I'm not so sure," Renee answered as she kept the cart rolling and watched the animal. Dog did seem a little shy, as if he was nervous around them.

Or maybe she just imagined he was that way because

she couldn't take any more stress right now, and if he wasn't growling or snapping at her, she didn't need to worry about him.

Inside the bunkhouse, Rusty heard a rumble and walked over to open the door for Renee and the young woman. He noted Renee gave him an odd look when she passed him, but he had no idea what it was for. Tessie was still sleeping on the sofa. While she was tossing and turning a bit, she was safe, so that couldn't be it. A gust of cold wind came inside and Rusty could see that heavy flakes were now falling. He suspected the snow might turn to rain soon. Their white Christmas might be more of an ice Christmas than anything.

By the time the tingle of the cold left his face, Rusty could smell the pot roast. He didn't blame the other men for stampeding to the table to take their places. His mouth was watering, too. He hadn't had a meal like this since— He stopped in thought. He couldn't remember.

The whirlwind of men reaching for the food as soon as it was on the table finally subsided, and in the wake of it, there were five places left in the circle, room for two people to sit on one side and three on the other. His brother sat down quick enough at one of the chairs and Karyn sat next to him.

That left a grouping of three chairs.

Rusty looked over at Renee. She seemed a little uptight as she studiously avoided his eyes. He wasn't about to wake up Tessie since, even with whatever adventures she was having in that dream that kept her tossing around, she had seemed tired to the bone. He saw no reason not to sit down and eat, though, so he walked over and pulled out a chair. He left two chairs on the one side so that Renee could choose to sit in a chair next to him or away from him.

Of course, she chose the one farthest from him. Rusty noticed everyone was looking around the table waiting for something.

"Sheriff Wall, would you mind saying the blessing for the food?" Renee finally asked.

The lawman gave a quick nod and the men and women bowed their heads.

"Father, we thank You for all You have provided for us today," the man prayed. "Keep us faithful. Keep us safe. Help us to live pleasing to You. Bless this food You have put before us. Amen."

Rusty couldn't help but wonder how the sheriff could pray with men he was intending to arrest. He could almost see the sheriff's mind working to figure out what had happened last night.

If Rusty hadn't seen his brother drive away, he would be wondering, too, if Eric had pulled the trigger of the gun that shot him. The boy had guilt written all over his face. And Rusty hadn't been around him much as the boy grew up. They had written and talked on the phone, but that was different from going fishing together and that kind of thing. Maybe Eric blamed Rusty for leaving him with their father when he went away to join the army.

The table was mostly silent as everyone ate. The roasted onions and garlic had flavored the slow-cooked beef, and the juices made the carrots and potatoes tender. Only the clink of the silverware on the plates was heard until Tessie groaned deeply in her sleep.

Rusty stood up instinctively to go to the girl, not noticing everyone else had stopped eating and was watching as Tessie's mother also left her chair to tend to her daughter.

"I'm sorry," Rusty muttered, stopping himself from bending down to comfort Tessie. Of course, that right belonged to her mother.

Renee sat down on the edge of the sofa and put out a hand to wake Tessie.

Rusty knew he should probably go back to the table, but he stood towering awkwardly over the two of them. He didn't know if there was anything he could do to soothe the little girl, but he wanted to be available if there was.

"She okay?" the sheriff asked from his chair at the table.

Rusty shot the lawman a grateful look even though he didn't answer. He would leave that to Renee.

At that moment, Tessie screamed and opened her eyes in terror.

"Daddy!" the girl called as she looked around the room frantically. "I thought my daddy was here."

"Oh, sweetie," Renee murmured as she tried to gather Tessie into her arms.

The girl squirmed away from her mother and scrambled off the sofa. Tessie looked around the room a second time before seeming to notice Rusty. Then she launched herself straight at him.

Rusty was stunned as Tessie stopped in front of him and lifted her arms. Her eyes were wide with fright and filled with tears.

"I want to see my daddy," Tessie commanded. "Take me to my daddy."

"I—ah," Rusty stammered as he bent down and lifted the girl into his arms. "Did you have a bad dream?"

Tessie nodded her head emphatically.

Rusty rubbed Tessie's back as he held her. "Just take a deep breath. Everything will be all right."

When the girl calmed a little, Rusty looked up and saw Renee staring at him as though he'd done something unpardonable.

"She's my daughter," Renee whispered, stricken. No one but Rusty could hear, but her words cut through his own panic. "Why doesn't she want to come to me? I'm her mother."

Rusty stepped closer to Renee and tried to pry Tessie away from him, but she had his neck in a lock that would do a wrestler proud.

"I want to see my daddy," she repeated to Rusty, her serious little face intent on him. "You know where he is. You can take me to him."

Rusty looked over to Renee in appeal and then turned back to the girl. "No, Tessie, I don't know where your father is. And I'm no prince. No castle. Nothing."

Looking at the girl's eyes, he couldn't tell whether she was imagining her father in some fantasy or if she wanted to see the real man, the one who had broken her heart.

"I know where your father is," Renee said then, her voice sympathetic but firm. "He's in the Montana State Prison in Deer Lodge. And he's going to be there a long time."

Tessie stopped crying. In fact, for one wrenching moment, Rusty thought the little girl had stopped breathing. He no longer tried to encourage her to leave his arms.

"What's a prison?" she asked. "Do they have castles there?"

"No, sweetie," Renee said. "A prison is a place where bad people go."

Tessie was silent at that, her frown deepening.

"I'm sorry," Rusty whispered to both the woman standing next to him and the child he held. "I had no idea."

Renee acknowledged his words with a curt nod. "I don't talk about it, for obvious reasons."

He could see she was ashamed.

"It's not your fault," Rusty assured her, wishing he had use of both of his arms. He settled for taking a step closer to her. "What he did is on him, not you."

Rusty sensed something different about the room and glanced up to see that the table was empty. The food was still on the plates, but the men had left to give Renee and him some privacy.

"I still want to see my daddy," Tessie finally said again, no hysteria in her voice now.

Rusty glanced at Renee. "Do you think—?"

Renee looked up at him, worry in her eyes. "I don't know. What do you think?"

Rusty was silent for a moment. He was touched that Renee had asked for his opinion and he wanted to be helpful.

"Maybe, if she wants to see him, that means she

needs to see him," Rusty said. "Have you ever taken her to visit him?"

Renee shook her head. "I haven't felt strong enough to do that. I haven't even gone myself."

"Has he asked to see her?"

"No," Renee said softly. "Not either one of us. I doubt he cares."

"If you need help, let me know," Rusty offered. "I could go with the two of you if you decide you're ready."

She studied him then, her brown eyes searching his.

"No one wants to visit that place," she said. "I can't ask you to do that."

"You didn't ask. I'm volunteering," he assured her. When she still seemed undecided, he added, "Consider it repayment for you saving my life. It's much better than me having a talk with Tessie."

A small smile curled the corners of her mouth. "You're right. Maybe it's not too much to ask, considering. I'm going to have to take that rug in to the dry cleaner's to get the bloodstains out."

"We'll take it to Miles City on the way to Deer Lodge," Rusty agreed, feeling lighter inside suddenly. "It's not too far. We could make it there and back in one day. And I'll pay for the cleaning."

He didn't know how the ranch hands knew it was all clear, but they quietly filed back into the room and sat down at their places. He thought he heard one of them sigh in relief, but he couldn't tell which one because the din of silverware took over.

"I guess we should finish eating, too," Renee said then and held out her arms for Tessie.

The girl went to her mother gladly this time. Rusty had no doubt Tessie had already gotten what she wanted from him—a promise he'd make sure she could see her father.

After Rusty sat back in his chair, he wondered if he would have offered to help Tessie if he didn't know the pain of missing a parent himself. When he was a boy, he would have climbed over hot rocks to see his mother again. He always felt empty because she hadn't said goodbye. It didn't really matter whether the parent was worth one's love or not. Sometimes it was only his or her absence that haunted a person.

All those years since his mother left him, he'd felt as if he'd let her down in some inexplicable way. Had she tired of him not eating his vegetables? Had he waited too long every day to make his bed? Had she ever loved him?

For the first time it occurred to him that maybe the reason he was so unsettled around women was because he was afraid of failing them, too. Oh, he could do the good-time thing. Women wanted to date him. To dance, go out to dinner. Have a few laughs. But when things looked as if they might get serious, he left. He never knew if he had it in him to make someone happy.

He looked over at Renee then. He didn't want to fail her. If they got closer, he likely would. She had settled Tessie in the chair between them and was dishing up her daughter's plate. She must have felt his gaze, because she looked up and smiled.

"Thank you," she whispered.

He almost didn't respond. He believed in keeping his promises, but he regretted making this one. Taking

Tessie and Renee to see her ex-husband could hurt them both, and Rusty wouldn't know how to make it better.

No, after they took the trip, he'd find a way to leave. Now that he thought about it some more, the trip could be very bad. The man might not agree to see them. He might curse at them if he did. Or worse yet, he might smile at them and say things he didn't mean, pretending to emotions he didn't feel. Rusty felt his hand clench into a fist just thinking about that.

Rusty wondered if he should try to talk to Tessie's father before they visited him. It would be better if the man just wrote a short note to Tessie, telling her where he was and that he would be ready to see her in a few years.

Rusty's fist stayed clenched. He would have hated to get a note like that from his mother.

He looked over Tessie's head at Renee again. Anything that pained the daughter would be felt by her mother, too.

Somehow he had started something in their lives. He wished he really were a prince and could make this Christmas happy for them.

Chapter Six

Renee's alarm clock buzzed the next morning and she reached across her sleeping daughter to turn it off. After their upset two nights ago and the terror her daughter had faced in her nap yesterday, Renee had decided she wasn't going to let Tessie sleep alone. She wanted to be right there if her daughter had more nightmares. Neither of them had woken in the night, even though Renee had stayed awake for hours watching over her child before falling asleep herself.

"Tessie, sweetie," Renee said as she put her hand on her daughter's back. She bent close and kissed the girl on her forehead. "We've only got a half hour before it's time to leave for Sunday school."

Tessie opened her eyes. "Is the prince coming with us?"

Renee nodded her head reluctantly.

Assured her hero would be present, Tessie scrambled out of bed. "I'm going to wear my new red dress. It sparkles—like a princess dress."

Renee smiled, but not happily. Tessie was supposed

to save the dress for Christmas, but Renee decided not to protest. It was a small thing.

She'd had no idea Tessie's feelings were rolling around inside her the way they had been yesterday when she'd had her nightmare. Renee hoped the trip to see her father would give the girl some peace. Maybe then she would stop spinning so many fantasy tales. If it didn't work, Renee didn't know what else to do.

Tessie went to brush her teeth and Renee headed for the kitchen.

Sunlight was streaming into the blue-and-white room when Renee put two slices of bread into the toaster. Then she pulled a jug of orange juice out of the refrigerator, put a jar of Mrs. Hargrove's homemade chokecherry jelly on the table and turned on the coffeemaker. Renee took a moment to listen as the grandfather clock in the living room chimed nine times. The thing she was going to miss most when she moved back to the cook's quarters was that old clock. A person could hear it throughout the house. She never would have expected chiming would make her feel so wistful. Until she got her job here, she'd lived in a car, in hotel rooms and anywhere she and her husband could find shelter. Only people who lived in regular homes knew the pleasure of a grandfather clock. She was saving as much of her wages as she could in hopes she could buy a house someday. If she ever managed that, she was going to buy a grandfather clock, too.

She went back to the bedroom and pulled on a black turtleneck and a gray A-line skirt. She liked the skirt because it had extra fabric that made the cloth sway when she walked. She put on a gold hip belt and gold hoop earrings. The skirt was long enough that it looked good with her black boots, too.

The smell of toast brought her back into the kitchen. Tessie was sitting at the table drinking her juice and using a spoon to smear jam on her piece of toast.

"Be careful you don't get any jelly on your pretty dress," Renee said as she went to the counter and brought back a banana and began peeling it.

"Pretty," Tessie agreed as she put the spoon back in the jelly jar. "Sparkly."

"You have enough now," Renee cautioned as she looked at the mound of jelly on her daughter's toast.

Renee sat down and buttered her piece of toast while Tessie ate part of the banana and drank more juice.

When they had finished eating, there was a knock at the door.

"The prince!" Tessie exclaimed as she bounced up from her chair and ran to let the man inside.

"Ask who it is first," Renee called out to her.

Tessie calmed down enough to do as she was told and Renee recognized the deep tones of Rusty's reply.

Tessie was looking at her with a question in her eyes, so Renee nodded.

"You can open the door," she said.

The sun shone behind Rusty, adding sheen to the black suit he wore. The suit jacket was open to make room for his sling. A crisp white shirt was under the suit, making Renee think he must have some way to detach the sling while he dressed. Either that or he'd had help from his brother, who had spent the night with him in the bunkhouse.

Rusty reached up to tip his Stetson gallantly. The

black hat had been brushed and cleaned since Renee saw it last, too. Even the band looked new.

"Good morning," he said and Renee felt a slight tremble go through her as Rusty squatted down to grin at her daughter.

Tessie beamed.

This wasn't good, Renee told herself. She'd always been a pushover for a man who dressed up like this, and when he was also kind to her daughter, she melted.

Then she heard Tessie gasp in excitement and saw the girl kneel down just inside the open door. She put out her hand, still covered with smudges of jelly. Renee couldn't understand what her daughter was doing until a gray wolf head appeared around the corner.

"Dog!" Tessie exclaimed as the animal opened its mouth near her fingers and started to lick.

"Tessie, bring your hand back!" Renee commanded breathlessly.

Her daughter was giggling by then and wiggling her fingers. The dog had finished moving his tongue over her hand and stepped back at Renee's words.

"It's all right," Rusty said. Renee only now noticed he had a hand on the dog's head. "He'd never hurt Tessie."

"He's part wolf!" she answered in disbelief. "You don't know what he'll do. Besides, Tessie thinks he's as safe as a puppy."

Renee looked at her daughter, searching for any indications of fear. She had thought being that close to a wolfhound would terrify the girl, given her fantasies about her father's castle. But her daughter didn't even appear shaken by the experience. For the first time in months, Renee began to hope that Tessie would overcome her fears.

"I raised Dog from a pup," Rusty said as he looked up from where he was. "Saved his life. I would never let him this near Tessie unless I knew he wouldn't hurt her."

When her daughter didn't move away, Renee took a deep breath. She realized it wasn't the wolf dog that Tessie trusted; it was the man. The girl had no reason for that blind faith, though, and it troubled Renee. Not that it was Rusty's fault or his dog's. She was Tessie's mother. It was her job to protect her daughter. And that included helping her figure out when it was safe to put her faith in someone else.

"I'm sorry," Renee said to her daughter's hero. "I know Dog might never hurt you, but he doesn't know Tessie. She doesn't know him. I'd like you to keep him away from her. She's just a little girl and she's too trusting."

Rusty nodded. "If that's what you want."

Then he signaled Dog, and the animal turned and loped off the porch, taking up a position by a tree a few yards away. He sat and faced Renee, looking chastised and mournful.

"I'll fix him some food before we leave," Renee said then, feeling she might have been too harsh. The dog certainly didn't look ready to growl or bite anyone. The poodle that Mrs. Elkton's friend brought over sometimes behaved far worse than this wolf dog.

"Pete already gave him something to eat," Rusty said as he stepped inside and closed the door so they couldn't see Dog.

"I'll give him an extra treat later, then," Renee said as she smiled down at her daughter, trying to be reassuring. "And you, young lady, need to go wash your hands before we go. Rinse them twice and use soap. Then brush your teeth again. And put a towel around the top of your dress so you don't get any water spots on it."

Tessie skipped off to the bathroom, her joy in the day undiminished.

Rusty and Renee were silent for a moment.

"I am sorry," Rusty said softly. "I never wanted to scare you."

Renee nodded. Her heartbeat was just now returning to normal. "I know. And I may have overreacted."

Rusty reached up and brushed a strand of hair off her cheek.

So much for her heart calming down, Renee thought as she stared up at him.

"You and me—we can't seem to get our steps to match, can we?" he said. "I'm either going too fast or—" He stopped.

"Don't even think it," Renee said. "You're never going too slow. You crash into the Elktons' porch with a bullet in you. Might still get arrested for rustling. Manage to win my daughter's heart. And it hasn't even been a full two days."

She smiled to take the sting out of her words and his eyes softened.

"Well, when you put it that way, I guess I have been busy," Rusty murmured as he caressed Renee's cheek.

She tried to answer, but her throat was dry and the words wouldn't come out. Heat stroked down her cheek where his fingers touched her, but icy fear still filled her heart.

She cleared her throat.

"You even manage to show up in a suit," she whispered. She was as bad as Tessie. Letting her emotions overcome her good sense. It was as if she was jumping out of an airplane without checking to see if her parachute was working.

He leaned down slightly and she was sure he was going to kiss her.

But he didn't. Instead, he looked away, his hand falling from her face.

He was silent for a moment and then spoke. "The suit belongs to Pete. He lent it to me."

"His funeral suit?" Renee asked, trying to pull herself back to earth. Fortunately, thoughts of that suit brought reality fast enough. "He doesn't wear it much."

Rusty opened the suit and examined the lining. "It does smell a little like mothballs. Oh, well. Eric insisted I wear one if I'm going to church this morning. He's got this thing in his head that the people there are going to be looking at me to see if he's good enough for his girlfriend."

"Oh." Renee swallowed. That would be her fault.

"I'm surprised Eric isn't going, too," she said. That would be a better idea. More what she had in mind.

"Yeah, well, he says he's not ready to do that," Rusty said. "Afraid the sheriff will try to get him to tell him who was with him the other night in the ravine."

"I don't suppose he's told you."

Rusty shook his head. "Said he didn't want to put me in any danger."

"That man tried to kill you," she protested. "I don't see how knowing his name could make it any worse."

"That's what I told my brother," Rusty said. "He didn't agree. Said this man is sneaky. And has friends in high places."

Renee wished she knew if there really had been another man out in the darkness the other night. Maybe the two Calhoun men were just trying to hide their crimes under a cloud of general suspicion about an unnamed, faceless stranger.

"Well, I hope Eric appreciates that you are wearing this suit for him," she finally said. They seemed to trust each other, so she guessed that meant Rusty didn't believe his brother would have shot him. Whether he was right or not, she didn't know.

"I can't think of anything more ridiculous than me trying to impress people by wearing a suit," Rusty said as he brushed off the front of his jacket, even though there was no need. "But Eric was intent on it and, well, I haven't done enough for my brother over the years."

"I know you said you hadn't been to Dry Creek since you left," Renee said, trying to get the full picture of their relationship. "But I don't understand why."

Rusty shook his head. "The old man promised to make trouble for the kid if I came back. It was his way of punishing me. Keeping his two sons apart helped him control us. I only called Eric on the phone when I knew he was alone. If my father answered for some reason, I hung up."

"Eight years is a long time," Renee said. "Maybe if you had called and talked to your father he would have changed his mind. People do."

Rusty shrugged. "Not my old man. It was what it was with him."

She was disheartened. Rusty hadn't made enough effort to see his brother in the years he was gone. Any closeness he showed now could be feigned. She didn't know why she was always drawn to the wrong kind of men, but apparently she was. One good turn did not make a trustworthy man. Rusty might not be nearly as caring as he appeared. Maybe she just didn't give the good guys a chance—like Betty's candidates. Barry Grover might be a very nice man. At least he wouldn't draw her and her daughter into a life of crime.

"Well, we better go," Renee said as she stepped over to the closet at the side of the foyer. She pulled out Tessie's purple parka and her own black one. Then she added wool scarves for both of them.

She eyed Rusty. "Don't you have a coat?"

"I only have my denim one and it's got that hole in it from the bullet," he answered. "I didn't think it was good for church."

"Here." Renee reached into the closet and pulled out another parka. "It's a spare Mr. Elkton told me I could use when I go out to the barn. There's a rip on the right sleeve, but it's warm. And I keep it clean."

"I don't need that sleeve anyway," Rusty said as he took the coat from her. "Thanks."

He slid his left arm into the coat and draped the rest over the arm with the cast.

"I wouldn't mind getting there early," Renee said as she helped him adjust the coat. "Eugene Wells and his wife have been driving out from Miles City to services. He's the lawyer I'd like to talk to."

Rusty raised an eyebrow. "I hope you're not planning to sue me for passing out the other night in front of your house."

Renee shook her head and then indicated Tessie, who had just come back. "I want to get custody arrangements all spelled out for someone special in case something happens to me."

"Oh." Rusty nodded and glanced down at Tessie. "Very important."

Renee finished pulling the hood on her daughter's head and then straightened. "If I'm going to see my ex-husband, I want to have the papers so he can sign right then. I don't want to make another trip."

"Will the attorney be able to draw them up by tomorrow? I was hoping we could leave then. I don't know what the sheriff has planned for my future, but I want to be sure we make this trip before anything else happens."

Renee's heart sank. He expected to be arrested. That should tell her something. She'd have to ask the sheriff if it was even safe for her and Tessie to drive to Deer Lodge with Rusty. She didn't want to say anything about that now, though.

"Knowing Eugene, he'll do the papers this afternoon," Renee said instead with a determined smile. "I don't know how he does it, but he's fast. Plus, he has some information already. We started the process when my ex-husband sent the divorce papers. I planned to have Eugene finish the documents in a few months, so he probably has them at least half-completed already."

Renee opened the door and ushered the three of them out. The pickup she was driving was right off the porch. Five inches of snow had fallen in the night and the only breaks in it were two sets of footprints from Rusty and his wolfhound. She looked over to where Dog had been sitting, but he was gone.

Renee was almost to the pickup when she noticed something.

"You scraped off the windshield!" she exclaimed to Rusty.

He nodded and reached over to open the door for her.

"You ever hear about the gangster who liked cats?" she asked as she slid into the driver's seat.

Rusty shook his head. Then he strapped Tessie into her booster chair in the backseat before climbing into the cab himself.

"Anything I should know?" Rusty asked when she turned the ignition.

She glanced over at him. "About what?"

She hoped he wasn't going to ask her what the sheriff thought.

"Churches," he said, surprising her. "I know sometimes they have different customs."

"Nothing unusual," Renee said as she backed up and made a loop onto the lane leading to the edge of the ranch property. "The Dry Creek church is like other traditional churches."

Rusty was silent, but he seemed so nervous she looked over at him. He was stoic, looking straight ahead. If it wasn't for the tenseness of his jaw, she wouldn't have suspected anything was wrong.

"You have gone to other churches, haven't you?" she asked as she made a turn onto the gravel county road.

He shook his head.

"Never?" she asked in astonishment, thankful the snowplow had been through already.

Rusty shrugged. "No."

Tessie's voice came from the backseat. "You can come to my Sunday school class with me. We have animal crackers and juice. Not grape juice because we might spill. But apple juice. And Mrs. Hargrove tells us stories from the Bible. There's no wolf dogs, but they have kings. And there's a lot of sheep. And some camels. I've never ridden a camel."

Renee noticed the grin on Rusty's face. He likely had never heard a young girl chatter away without pause. Nor did he realize it meant Tessie liked him.

"The adults meet with coffee at the back of the church," Renee informed him when her daughter took a breath. "We have a Bible study going on the book of Psalms. Talking about how to praise God when times are hard."

Rusty nodded. "My chaplain gave me a copy of the Psalms."

Renee put her foot on the brake and looked over at him. "You have a chaplain?"

She tried not to be surprised. But she didn't think many criminals had a chaplain before they were sent to prison.

"He's the army's chaplain," he said with a slight smile. "He—helped me."

Renee knew that pause told a story, but she wasn't sure she wanted to know what it was. She put her foot on the gas and the pickup started moving again. She needed some distance between herself and this man. She was having a hard time remembering why he was so unsuited to her. Even if he had been stealing cattle, maybe it was a onetime thing. Maybe he could change. Maybe— She made herself stop.

She wasn't going down that road with another man. Her ex-husband had been enough. No more making everything look better than it was. Of course, her ex-husband had never read a Bible or considered going to a church except for the time he tried to figure out how he could rob the collection plate when it was being passed. His plan involved Tessie tipping over the plate, and Renee had never forgiven him for even thinking of involving their daughter in a crime. At least Rusty had that much in his favor; he'd never tried to use Tessie.

Of course, she forced herself to consider, Rusty might not be telling the truth about everything. He might not have a chaplain. Might not care about Tessie. Or Dog. Maybe it was all just a cover for the crimes he and his brother had committed.

She didn't even know if he was telling the truth about not visiting Eric in the past eight years. Maybe they'd spent months together preparing to rustle the cattle that were missing around here. If the sheriff was right, they both had reason to resent the local ranchers after their own ranch had been taken away. She'd heard low whispers in the hardware store that some ranchers might suffer foreclosure if the rustling wasn't stopped soon. Maybe the Calhoun brothers were out for revenge.

"Okay, we're in Dry Creek," Renee announced, the cheer in her voice so artificial she almost winced. She realized suddenly that, even if she didn't know this man's past or future crimes, she knew someone who did.

Father, give me wisdom around him, she prayed silently, her eyes open and watching the road. *I need to protect Tessie. And my own heart. Give the sheriff the knowledge he needs to arrest Rusty if he has done something wrong or is planning something illegal. And above all, keep my Tessie safe. Amen.*

"Everything looks the same," Rusty said as he looked down the street.

Fortunately, he seemed focused on the church building and she didn't think he was aware of how stressed she had suddenly become.

The white church was just as Rusty remembered it, although it must have been painted at least once since he'd left Dry Creek, because it seemed brighter than the other buildings around it.

The church was set on a cement basement, and ground-level windows were scattered along the walls. Tufts of dried grass poked up from the layer of snow by the basement walls. A half dozen cement stairs, with black metal handrails, led up to a square landing outside the weathered oak double doors. More windows were set in the upper part of the building. Renee parked the pickup beside the church and Rusty automatically stepped out and opened the back door so he could get Tessie and take her inside. There was no sidewalk from the parking places to the steps and with all the snow and slush around, Tessie would get her shiny black shoes dirty if he didn't carry her.

A few flakes of snow were still falling as he climbed the stairs with Tessie in his arms. Renee opened the door for them all. A burst of warm air greeted them when they stepped inside. A rack for coats ran along one wall, complete with a bench beneath it for people to sit and take off their snow boots. Colorful mittens and scarves were piled on a shelf on top of the rack.

Instinctively, he checked for an orange parka among the coats, but didn't find one. There was one with an orange lining, but it looked like a woman's coat since it had a fluffy knit scarf tucked under the collar—the kind of scarf, with huge billowing ruffles down the side, that no man would ever wear.

Rusty put Tessie down and took his hat off. That was been one thing he'd learned about churches from his mother. She always said a gentleman never wore a hat when he had tea with the queen or when he visited a church. Rusty couldn't imagine doing either as a boy, so he'd kept his hat on his head most of the time.

Renee took Tessie's parka and found a hook for it before he pulled off her red mittens.

Suddenly Rusty became aware that the noise level had dropped and he turned around. A good number of the people in the church had stopped milling around and were looking at him.

"They're damp," he assured everyone as he lifted up the small knit mittens. "And I am going to lay them flat on the rack up there."

Apparently, the sight of a Calhoun male in their church was astonishing to people. They certainly were staring. Not looking unfriendly, exactly, just dumbfounded.

He wondered if the boys had spread the word about his mean face. Or maybe it was the mittens. Surely some of the men standing there helped their children take their mittens off at times like this.

And then it hit him. Of course they had helped their children, but Tessie wasn't his daughter. He'd forgotten how these subtle things were noticed in a small town. And he hadn't intended his actions to proclaim any feelings for Renee, because he knew she wouldn't like it. And he wasn't in a position to be attached anyway. But he could hardly put the mittens back on the girl's hands.

Finally he saw Mrs. Hargrove across the room. She was talking to someone, but she waved and started to walk toward him, a large brown paper bag that had a red logo from a store in her hands.

He waved back at her and quickly put the mittens on the shelf.

When he turned around, he saw most people had stopped looking at him directly, but he could tell they were keeping an eye on him. He stared right back at the few who were still openly watching. But he could see all of them. Men in denim jeans and buttoned-up cotton shirts, some with vests and some with ties. Twenty or so women dressed in casual slacks and sweaters.

"Maybe I shouldn't have worn a suit," Rusty whispered to Renee. "Nobody else here is wearing one."

"Pastor Curtis wears one."

Rusty nodded. "Great. Now they're all going to think I'm putting on airs."

Mrs. Hargrove stood in front of Rusty and Renee. Tessie had warmed up by now and was on her way to her basement Sunday school class.

"I'm so glad you came," the older woman said as she looked up at Rusty.

Rusty nodded. "Everyone's staring at me."

"Oh, that," Mrs. Hargrove said with a light laugh. "They're waiting for me to give you your costume. They want to be sure you're still going to be King Herod."

"I said I would," Rusty assured her.

"I was going to try your costume on in our practice this afternoon," Mrs. Hargrove said as she turned to rummage in her bag. "But we have to cancel practice because a big storm is coming this way. And Beth Ann, who is the one making alterations on the costumes, needs to get your measurements so she can make any adjustments this afternoon. We want you to be comfortable. Ah!" she exclaimed as she started pulling something out of the bag. "Let's see how this fits."

Mrs. Hargrove held out a shining purple bathrobe.

Rusty stepped back. "You can't— I can't— I mean, that's a woman's robe."

"Well, not anymore," the older woman said calmly. "I believe it belongs to the church."

"The church wears black lace?" Rusty asked doubtfully as Mrs. Hargrove held one arm of the purple robe up to him. It wasn't just the collar that had lace, either, Rusty thought. There was lace on the cuffs and a big patch of the stuff on the back of the robe. This wasn't just a woman's robe; it was a lady's garment.

"I'm pretty sure kings wore lace once upon a time," Mrs. Hargrove explained. "Remember that and you'll be fine."

Rusty looked out at the crowd that had gathered by now. He could see the amusement in the eyes of the men and the pity in the eyes of the women. He gave them his mean look.

"I'm going to wear my hat," Rusty declared. He wasn't going to let Mrs. Hargrove down, but he wasn't going to let them add anything more to his misery. "No crown jewels or anything like that. If I put jewelry with that robe in front of the whole town, I'll never be able to drive down the street in Dry Creek again."

"So you'll wear it?" the older woman asked. "For the pageant."

Rusty had no choice. He kept his promises. "That's the way it looks."

A spattering of applause broke out among the people watching him. Before he knew it, a young woman with a tape measure in one hand and a book of pins in the other was standing behind him. She pressed the back of the robe against him shoulder to shoulder and muttered something about inches.

"I think I can make it fit," she announced. "If we need more room, we can always cheat and cut a small slit in the neckline where the collar is."

Beth Ann gave the robe back to Mrs. Hargrove and the older woman put it back in her bag.

"I'll keep it for our Tuesday morning practice," Mrs. Hargrove said as she opened her purse slightly and raised her voice. "Remember everyone—I'm canceling our practice for today."

"We only have one more practice, then?" Renee asked as she stood beside him in silence.

Mrs. Hargrove had looked down to search her purse. Finally, she pulled out a white sealed envelope that she held out to Rusty. "Here. These are your lines. Renee will help you learn them."

Rusty felt he was good and well corralled.

That was when he heard a noise behind him. With all of the commotion going on around him, he didn't know why that noise stood out, but it did. Someone had been back by the coat hooks. Rusty looked around. No one was where the sound had come from, but the coats had been moved. And he no longer saw the parka with the orange lining hanging anywhere.

Before he could puzzle out what happened, Sheriff Wall was standing next to him.

"Problems?" the lawman asked.

Rusty looked away from the coats and focused on the sheriff. "Not that I know of."

"Humph," the sheriff snorted slightly. "Well, I came to talk to you anyway, about going to see Renee's ex-husband."

Rusty noted that Renee had stepped far enough away that she couldn't hear their conversation. She was talking to an older couple. The man carried a briefcase and Rusty figured he was the lawyer she had wanted to ask about paperwork for her custody issues. He saw the man nod, so it looked as though everything was lining up nicely.

"We're planning to go on Monday," Rusty told the sheriff, keeping his voice low. "I was going to tell you. I didn't know until a second ago that the day would work."

"I've given it some thought," the lawman continued with a nod, not seeming to care who might overhear his words. "I think her ex-husband might know something about the rustling that is going on. It's all happening in the northeast corner of the state. That's where he committed his crimes."

"I thought he was in for robbery," Rusty responded, not sure what point the sheriff was trying to make.

"Rustling is robbery," the sheriff insisted. "And he hasn't been in prison for so long that he's lost his connections. Thieves tend to hang together, or at least know where they are so they don't step on each other's toes."

"Okay, maybe," Rusty agreed. He could see the lawman's logic.

"So I figure if you strike up a conversation with him," Sheriff Wall continued, "he might tell you what he knows."

"Me?" Rusty asked. "He's going to tell me?"

"Well, it's not like he knows you," the sheriff said. "But he had accomplices he worked with. He likes to brag. Maybe we can make him think it will do him good to share his moves with a fellow thief."

"I'm not—"

The sheriff held up his hand. "We'll make up a back-story and feed it into the prison gossip vine. I know the warden there."

"I don't know if that will work," Rusty said, wondering when he could step away from this conversation. He knew how gossip grew. An overheard word there. A misunderstood word later.

"You have to try," the sheriff said with a glance over at Renee. "If we don't find out who's stealing those cattle, people will always wonder if it was you. Even if the rustling stops tomorrow."

Rusty followed the lawman's gaze over to Renee. The man was right. He might not have much of a future here, but he would like Renee to think well of him. Of course, that would never happen if she heard the gossip the sheriff was planning to start.

"Not this way," Rusty said as he turned back to the sheriff. "If the man just up and tells me, that's one thing. But I don't want rumors started."

Sheriff Wall shook his head. "All I'm asking is to set you up with a microphone before you go. You'll need permission to visit Renee's ex-husband anyway. The warden will help with that. All you have to do is give me the go-ahead and I'll get a microphone small enough to wear on your tie."

"Even if I do agree to the microphone, I'm not going to prison wearing a suit," Rusty said.

The sheriff chuckled. "Then I should be able to find a place in your sling."

They stood together a moment in silence.

"He's not likely to talk, though, unless he thinks you're a criminal," the sheriff finally said. "Think about what I've said. It won't take long to set up a rumor in the prison."

"I don't think I'll change my mind," Rusty said. "I know how far gossip reaches. My reputation is about all I've got."

Just then someone started playing the organ at the front of the church and everyone got quiet and started to walk toward the pews.

Rusty almost turned and walked out of the church. He felt as if he'd been through turmoil already this morning. He'd been tempted, ridiculed and forced to give up his pride to help an older woman, and he'd been asked to give up his good name.

But then he saw Renee turn in a pew and search for him. He kept his eyes on her and walked down the aisle to where she was sitting.

"Mind if I—?" he asked.

"Not at all," she said with a cool smile as she moved down to give him more room. "I don't own the church."

And with that, she offered her hymnal to him so he could share.

She had a beautiful voice, he thought as he listened to her sing "Amazing Grace." Everyone was singing, but her voice came through with a purity that could only come from conviction. He wondered if he would ever have that kind of grace in his life. He knew the message of the song. The chaplain had seen to that. But forgiveness like that didn't seem possible in this life, not even from God. He had let too many people down to wipe those actions under some kind of heavenly rug and pretend they had never happened.

Chapter Seven

Renee had tears in her eyes by the time Pastor Curtis had finished the sermon. His words on the prodigal son touched her once again as she contemplated how far a person could fall in this life and still be forgiven by God.

She had been at the bottom of her existence the night she came back to Dry Creek almost a year ago, with poor little Tessie sleeping in the backseat of her rundown car. Her husband was robbing another gas station and she had driven away. The back window didn't even close and she remembered how the shrill whistle of the wind through the crack sounded so loud that she worried her husband would find them.

She'd been frantically looking for the Elkton ranch because the last she'd heard, her father had been the foreman of the place. She'd followed road after road, always turning when she saw another pair of headlights. Afraid of her husband and the man he'd found to work with him, she drove fast and erratically. It was not surprising to her that she never found the massive welcome gate over the dirt lane that led to the Elkton ranch that night.

She had ended up on Gracie Stone's porch instead, confused and almost unconscious from the blood she had lost. One of the first people she'd seen, after Gracie and her father, had been Sheriff Wall. She remembered the sharp bark of his questions that night and how safe they made her feel.

The man had been doing his job and she'd trusted him. It was only when she felt better that she resented being arrested.

The pastor asked everyone to stand for the benediction. As Renee stood, she glanced across the aisle and saw the sheriff there with his wife and children. His stocky frame seemed a little shrunken today in his black denim jeans and plaid cotton shirt. His plain, square face was serious. The hair on his balding head appeared a little sparser than usual. For some reason, he looked as if the weight of the world was pressing down on his shoulders. And in a way, the troubles in this part of the world likely were.

Renee bowed her head as the organ played softly and the pastor blessed everyone, asking God to watch over each of them during the coming week. The affection in the pastor's voice when he prayed for his people always brought tears to Renee's eyes. This little town might not be much on the map, but no one could stay here long and claim he or she was not loved by this church.

When Renee lifted her head, she looked around. The day was still overcast, but some light came through the side row of windows made of vintage bubbled glass.

She made her way past a few of the people walking down the aisle until she stood next to the sheriff.

"I want to apologize for my words the other night," she said to him quietly. "About the arrest and all. You had no choice but to take me into custody. I don't want you to think I have hard feelings."

Renee smiled past the sheriff to the man's wife, Barbara. The dark-haired woman had brought her daughter and son to Dry Creek some years ago while her husband had also been serving a prison term. Since she'd married the sheriff, her children had grown in confidence and character. Neither of them had developed a problem with denial, the way Tessie had, either. Renee decided to sit down and have a long conversation with Barbara someday soon.

She looked back at the sheriff and he was searching her eyes for something.

"I don't want to bring you bad news like that ever again," he said as he glanced over her shoulder. "But my job is to keep you and your daughter safe. I will do what I have to."

"Even break our hearts?" she asked softly.

He nodded grimly.

"I appreciate it," Renee said with a slight smile. "You were looking out for me back then, too."

With that, she saw the sheriff shift his attention. He was no longer talking to her; he had on his official face and was focused on someone behind her.

"I forgot to give you something," the lawman said to that person as he reached into this pocket. He pulled out a Ziploc bag with a scrap of paper inside and held it out. "I never called the number."

Renee turned slightly so she could see Rusty reach out and take the bag.

"I don't care if you do call the number," he said. "But I appreciate having it back. That's the number for my chaplain."

The sheriff looked as stunned as Renee had been when Rusty first told her he had a minister in his life.

"You talk to this chaplain?" the sheriff asked casually. "I know sometimes people have a number for someone—say, a dentist—but that doesn't mean they have ever used the person's services. You know what I mean?"

Now, that, Renee told herself, was why she needed people like the sheriff around her. She'd never even considered that.

Rusty chuckled without much humor. "Oh, I talk to the man, all right. According to him, he digs around inside my soul and finds things—bringing them up to the light, or so he says." Rusty paused a moment and continued, fondness in his voice, "It's no wonder I lost his number."

"You didn't lose it," Renee said in a rush. "I took it out of your pocket."

"And gave it to the sheriff?" Rusty turned to her in amazement.

"Well, I wasn't going to keep it," she said to defend herself. "And you were a suspect. A lot of cattle have been stolen lately."

Rusty shook his head. "I guess I should have known after the shirt."

"What shirt?" the sheriff asked on sudden alert.

Renee blushed. "I had to check him out to see if he

had a gun hidden. Of course, his shirt was there. Right on his back where it was supposed to be."

Fortunately, the lawman nodded at that explanation. "I thought maybe there was another shirt. Something with evidence."

"No, just the one shirt," Rusty said. "I've borrowed the other clothes I've worn from Pete. I left my duffel with the rest of my clothes in the hayloft at my family's old ranch. The place is deserted. No tools left in the barn and dust all over the house. The hay left in the loft will mold before long."

"The farm tools were sold at auction," the sheriff said. "And I don't think the new owners intend to use the buildings. The hay probably isn't worth moving for them."

Rusty nodded. "It's a solid place. Too bad they're going to leave it to rot. The house wasn't even locked. The furniture's still inside. I didn't go upstairs, but I expect the bedroom closets still have clothes in them."

"No one bid on the sofa and chairs in the auction," the sheriff said. "It didn't seem right somehow. I doubt anyone wanted the clothes."

"Someone apparently wanted that new Case IH tractor my father bought three years ago," Rusty said. "Has a smooth ride. I didn't see that anywhere around."

Renee had been going to step away, but that remark kept her in place. If he knew how the tractor rode, did that mean he'd been back at the ranch before the auction?

"I'm not sure what the corporation that bought the place has done with anything," the sheriff continued.

Rusty nodded. He looked tired to her.

"Before I came to church, I got some information back from the call Betty made to the sheriff in Havre," the sheriff said then. "They didn't have much on you, except your birth date and that you were in the army. They checked further and found you'd gotten a medal of some kind for saving your fellow soldiers in some explosion in Afghanistan."

"I'm not the one who deserves a medal," Rusty said, his voice low and tinged with pain.

Renee could tell he would rather go back to talking about farm equipment or his shirt than the medal he'd earned.

"Are you sure your duffel will be safe over there?" Renee asked. "You could borrow a ranch pickup and go get it if you want."

"Thanks," Rusty said, his voice returning to normal. "Pete said the same thing. I might do that later this afternoon."

Renee nodded. People were starting to leave the church.

"Excuse me," she said to the two men. "I want to say hello to my dad and Gracie before they hurry back home. If I know Gracie, she has something in the oven. And I need to check on Tessie, too."

The sheriff nodded and he and his family started down the aisle. By that time, her father and his wife were walking up the aisle toward her, with Tessie between them. Her father was limping a little from the fall he'd taken a few months ago, the pain of his movements adding a few lines to his still smiling face. Gracie's long black hair was wound in a braid at the back of her neck and she wore a pretty yellow cotton dress.

Rusty stood beside her, so she had no choice but to introduce him to the older couple when they drew close.

"Dad, Gracie," she greeted the two and gestured toward Rusty, "you've probably heard about the man who came to the Elkton ranch for help the other night. Rusty Calhoun."

"He has a wolf dog," Tessie whispered in excitement as she squeezed their hands. "He licked me."

"She had jelly on her fingers," Renee explained.

"Dog usually has better manners," Rusty said as he reached out his left hand to her father. "Sorry. My regular shaking hand is in this sling. But I'm pleased to meet you."

He then turned to Gracie and nodded. "Ma'am."

"Tessie is quite excited about your dog," Gracie said with a smile. "That's all she's talked about since she came up the stairs from Sunday school."

Renee was relieved her daughter wasn't still talking about castles and princes.

"We heard you were in some trouble," her father said, leaning forward to be sure to catch what Rusty had to say.

"I owe your daughter my life," Rusty agreed, nodding at her father.

"I just did what anyone would do," Renee protested and then looked over at Gracie. "No more than what you did for me last Christmas."

"It was the best surprise of all," Gracie said as she smiled over at Renee. "I gained a daughter and a granddaughter."

The older woman looked down at Tessie fondly.

"You've been good to us," Renee said, her voice solemn. She didn't know what was wrong with her today. Everything seemed to make her teary eyed.

Renee blinked and Gracie reached over and squeezed her arm. "I expect all of this reminds you of how scared you were back then."

Maybe that was it, Renee told herself in relief.

Gracie turned to Rusty and gave him an approving nod. "I see you're all fixed up. If you need some salve to help your scars heal, let me know."

Rusty shot a questioning look toward Renee.

She shook her head slightly at him. "She's talking about the scar from where you were shot."

Rusty looked back at Gracie and nodded. "I'd be grateful."

Almost everyone had left the church by now and Renee could hear the sounds of pickups and cars being started outside. She heard some rattling, too, which meant the wind had started to blow stronger. The light coming in the windows had lessened.

"We'd love to have you come over for dinner," Gracie said graciously, including Renee and Rusty both in her invitation. "It's not much, but I did make a pumpkin pie yesterday to go with our spaghetti."

"I need to put the meal on the table in the bunkhouse," Renee said. "Karyn usually does it, but she said she had something else to do today. It's not much, either," she assured Gracie. "Last night I took a batch of my spicy Mexican chili out of the freezer to thaw and I have some corn bread ready to mix when I get there."

"Nothing like chili on a cold day like today," her father said approvingly. "That's been a favorite in the bunkhouse since I can remember."

"Well, I hope you don't mind if Tessie comes home with us for a few hours," Gracie said. "We'll bring her back this evening."

"Please!" Tessie added her own plea. "Grandma and Grandpa have new kittens."

"That we do," Gracie agreed with a smile at the girl. "But I hear you want a puppy instead."

Tessie nodded. "But I like kitties, too."

"Fair enough," Gracie said as she looked back at Renee. "Is that okay? I know it's close to Christmas and you may have plans."

"Not today," Renee said. "In fact, it will give me a chance to get some other things done."

Renee bent down and gave her daughter a kiss on her forehead. "You do what Grandma and Grandpa say, now, understand?"

Tessie nodded her head vigorously and her eyes shone with excitement.

With that Renee's father and stepmother turned and started walking down the aisle to reach the back of the church, Tessie skipping along between them.

Renee and Rusty stood watching them for a moment.

"I miss her already," Renee said with a smile up at Rusty. "She doesn't leave me often."

"It's hard to compete with kittens," Rusty consoled her.

Renee smiled at that. "I don't know what I'd do if they had puppies. I'd never see her."

"Well, I'm sure we can think of something to do today to keep your mind off your loneliness," Rusty said as he offered her his left elbow to hold on to. When she looked at him, puzzled, he added, "I'm guessing the steps are already icy out there. No point in ruining a good day with a fall."

They walked to the door and agreed that the weather was very cold. New snow hadn't started to fall yet, although gusts of wind were stirring up what snow was already on the ground.

Renee held on to his arm as they walked down the steps and headed to the pickup. This time when they arrived, Rusty took the scraper and quickly ran it over the bottom half of the windshield.

"The only snow that's on there came from the wind blowing," he said as he climbed into the pickup cab after Renee had started the engine.

They were the last ones to drive away from the church and Renee decided the day might be enjoyable after all. The cab warmed up quickly and the roads were only beginning to drift over.

Rusty knew the routine by the time they got back to the bunkhouse, and he set the table for Renee while she stirred up the corn bread in the kitchen. She said she also had an apple crisp made the day before that she was going to heat for dessert. He noticed the ranch hands looking at him with curiosity on their faces.

"She hire you or something?" Pete finally asked from his perch on the bench by the fireplace. He had a knife out and was doing some whittling. Rusty looked for a pile of shavings, but there were none, so he figured the other man was merely smoothing out some work he'd already done.

"No," Rusty said with a shake of his head as he circled the table with white bowls that he put at each place. "Worse than that. She saved my life."

The other man considered those words. "I suppose that does put you under some obligation." He paused. "But anyone would do the same."

"Then I'd be laying out dishes on their table," Rusty agreed. "I believe in paying my debts."

"Well, I can't argue with that," Pete said as he set his whittling aside and stood up. "Next time head for the bunkhouse, though. The most we'd make you do is muck out some of the horse stalls."

"I'll remember that," Rusty noted. "It's been some time since I was around livestock, but a man never forgets the pleasure of working with animals."

Pete eyed him for a bit. "A ranch boy never forgets much of anything."

Rusty nodded but didn't say anything. He wished he could wipe from his memory some things about his days on the ranch. He didn't consider remembering to be as important as some others might. Life with his father had been no stroll by a mountain brook.

"I reckon you know most everything there is to know about ranching," Pete added, walking closer to the table where Rusty was working. "I've been on the place your father used to have. You had lots of acreage."

"All bought and paid for by my great-grandparents," Rusty said. He didn't like to give the impression to people that his father had been the one to pay for the ranch. He'd inherited it just the way his parents had done.

Pete finally said what Rusty figured he had been leading up to for the past few minutes. "Mr. Elkton is looking for a new foreman. You might think about applying."

Rusty stopped at that.

"Don't any of the men here want the job?" he asked.

Most of them were ranch boys, too. Rusty knew that much from his conversation with them this morning. The custom was that Sunday was the cook's morning off and the men made do with bowls of cornflakes for breakfast. When Rusty got up, he'd decided he'd rather have some eggs and bacon, and since Renee had already told him that those were some of the things she always bought plenty of, he decided to get a frying pan hot and make himself some. He used a little flour, milk and eggs to make himself some pancake batter, too.

By the time he was halfway through cooking his breakfast, a line had formed outside the cookhouse door with men looking for a handout.

Once a man got cooking, it wasn't that hard to fry up a few more eggs and pancakes, so he kept on making breakfast until everyone was full.

He liked to think he'd made a few friends this morning using a spatula, and he didn't want to snatch away a job that one of them had his eye on.

"Well, now," Pete said as he ran his hand along his chin in thought. "It's not that easy to be foreman. You got to set up the work schedules, which means the foreman almost always has someone upset with him. And you have to take the lead on the branding in the fall and the calving in the spring. Means late nights."

Pete paused. "The truth is those of us working now are all in our forties and up. Now, we're good workers, don't get me wrong. But a man in his twenties might have more drive than the rest of us."

Rusty considered what Pete was telling him. "You're not just saying that because you know I don't have a job or anywhere else to go?"

"We're not running any charity outfit, if that's what you're asking. And it's Mr. Elkton that would have the final say anyway. We'd be happy to put in a good word for you if you want us to."

Rusty grinned. "I wouldn't say no. I've missed Montana. There's nothing like looking out as far as a man can see and finding nothing but grass and sky."

Rusty stood a moment enjoying the place. He felt surrounded by goodwill and friends. He could hear the storm starting outside, but a steady heat was coming from the fireplace as the embers of a large log glowed in the afternoon.

Then he heard the sound of the cart Renee used to bring the food over to the bunkhouse. Metal grated as wheels rolled over the wood planks.

"Let's not mention it to—" Rusty said.

He didn't even finish before Pete nodded. "Right. Give her time to get used to you before you tell her you might be staying. Women like to take things slow."

Rusty wasn't sure time was the problem here, but he nodded as he walked over to open the door for Renee. He almost told her about the job possibility the minute he saw her face. Her cheeks were red from the cold and she looked merry. Instead, he helped her pull the cart into the room before she stepped back out to the porch and rang a gong.

"I had no idea you had a dinner bell," Rusty said when she came back inside.

Renee shrugged. "It beats screaming for everyone to come."

The doors along the hallway opened, one after another, and six ranch hands came out, half of them smoothing down their hair as though they'd just gotten up from a nap. Rusty had slept in one of the other rooms last night and the right-end one was empty.

Rusty helped Renee put the pots of chili and platters of corn bread on the table. The men all took their places and this time Renee asked Pete if he would say grace for the meal.

The men bowed their heads.

When the prayer was over, Rusty helped pass bowls of chili around the table. Renee had plates of chopped onions and cheese for those who wanted to add them to their chili.

Everyone was dished up when Renee spoke.

"Someone did the breakfast dishes," she said. "And I want to thank them. I appreciate that you give me and Tessie Sunday mornings to sleep in, but I know cold cereal isn't your favorite. So I want to know who to thank."

Rusty looked around at the men. Most of them had spoons full of chili halfway to their mouths.

"We didn't have cold cereal," Pete confessed.

"You didn't eat breakfast?" Renee said in surprise. "I know you don't like the cereal much, but you should eat something."

"We had bacon and eggs," Pete said then. "And pancakes."

It was silent for a moment.

"He made them," Pete finally said with a jerk of his hand, indicating Rusty.

Renee turned to him as if he had fed them wild mushrooms. "You cook?"

"A little," he said with a shrug. "If there's a problem with the supplies, I'll pay for them."

"Of course you don't need to pay," Renee said, still looking a little dazed. "It's just that none of the men have ever cooked anything. I could be out there in the cookhouse, sick in bed and running a fever, and they won't open a can of soup."

"Well, we—" Pete began.

"I'm not saying it's your job," Renee interrupted. "I'm only saying I'm surprised Rusty can cook—and is willing to do it. That's all."

Rusty grinned. "I'm good with a barbecue grill, too. Make my own sauce."

"Maybe come springtime, we can—" Pete started and then stopped. He bent over his bowl of chili then and started to eat.

Rusty didn't respond. Renee didn't look as if she attached any meaning to the ranch hand's words, anyway. He was starting to have hope. His home was in Dry Creek. He knew that now. He'd never thought he'd live in this area again. With his family's ranch gone, he had nowhere to live—until today.

And then there was Renee. He was drawn to her. There was no doubt about that. He watched her now as she talked with the others at the table. She was kind. Passionate about her daughter. A perfect woman.

But he didn't know if they had a future together.

He'd never pictured himself marrying. Deep down, he wasn't sure he wouldn't disappoint her if she married him. As with his mother, he would be always wondering if he didn't make enough money, didn't keep his socks well organized enough or didn't do some fool thing he didn't even know he was supposed to do. He just didn't know.

Chapter Eight

Renee rolled over in bed and drew the quilts closer to her shoulders. The clock said it was seven o'clock in the morning, but it was still dark outside. Not pitch-black, but the heavy gray darkness let her know before she even looked out the frosted windows that a lot of snow had fallen last night. She was glad her father had phoned and said they thought it best to keep Tessie overnight. The roads might have been blocked if they had tried to bring her back after supper when they had planned.

Renee knew the trip to Deer Lodge would need to be postponed for a day. The blizzard was supposed to ease up by midmorning and the county crews would be out with their plows the minute the snowflakes stopped. But until then, she had to get dressed and walk over to the bunkhouse so she could make breakfast for the men. They'd be hungry—as always.

She had to admit that sometimes she found it a re-lentless job to put three meals on the table every day for the ranch hands, but her work allowed her to keep Tessie with her. The two of them ate with the men, so she didn't have the extra chore of cooking for her own small family.

Of course, her dream of having a home of her own was growing stronger.

If that ever happened, she'd enjoy preparing special meals for her daughter. Sometimes she felt as if there should be another adult at the table when she did so, but no one's face ever appeared in her mind when she imagined it.

Renee dressed in a fleece top and her flannel-lined jeans. She tucked her jeans into heavy work boots that came up to her knees. It wasn't far to the bunkhouse from the main house, but she put on her parka and wrapped two scarves around her—one around her neck and another over her nose like a bandanna. The fuzzy yarn kept her face warm and she could breathe through the loose stitches of the scarf.

The snow was eight inches deep when she opened the door, but she was prepared. She kicked it away from the door so none would seep into the house if it melted. The night had shed some of its dark while she dressed and she could see a dim light in the main room of the bunkhouse. Someone had turned the lamp on by the sofa.

She had no sooner stepped off the porch than she heard a whimper next to her. Through the snow she could see Dog was coming to walk beside her. She eyed the animal suspiciously, but he seemed friendly. The farther they walked the more she wondered if he had been waiting for her.

"Thought I might need some help, did you?" she asked the dog finally.

Dog gave a soft bark that she chose to think of as agreement. Fortunately, she had some meat scraps in the freezer at the bunkhouse. She'd been saving them for soup, but Dog might as well have them. She'd add some water and heat them up for him while she made breakfast for the men. She might even add a bone or two if she could find them.

A gust of wind, stronger than the regular force of the blizzard, blew suddenly and loose snow swirled in the air. Renee reached up to pull her scarf higher until all that showed was her eyes.

By the time she reached the porch of the bunkhouse, she realized she'd been walking with her hand on Dog's head and he was leading her. It wasn't that she couldn't find her way, she assured herself. It was just that all the blowing snow made it difficult. Even the light from the lamp was hidden from view. She figured someone must have turned it off.

But when Renee opened the door to the bunkhouse, the lamp was giving off the same soft glow as always. At least, she thought so. Snow had fallen on her eyelashes and she couldn't see inside the room very well. She stood waiting for the snow to melt.

She didn't want to wake the ranch hands earlier than necessary on a morning like this, but she did need to light the fireplace. Breakfast would be much more pleasant if everyone's fingers weren't stiff and cold.

After some of the snow had melted, she blinked and looked up, surprised to see Eric and Karyn sitting on the sofa, looking cold and miserable. A well-worn beige duffel bag sat next to Eric. Both teenagers had snow crusted on their boots and damp patches on their coats where frost or snowflakes had no doubt melted. Fortunately, the furniture in the bunkhouse would dry with no ill effects.

"Did you drive over?" Renee asked the young woman. Usually Karyn's brothers dropped her off. "I have a spare sweatshirt and jeans in the cook's quarters that I think would fit you if you want to change. Sitting around in damp clothes isn't good in this kind of weather."

"I'm the one who drove over," Eric said, his voice clipped. He was clearly upset, sitting there in a tight ball of anger. "Karyn just came with me."

The teenager was having a hard time keeping his raw emotion inside.

Renee wondered for a moment if she had stepped into a goodbye scene. She knew the two of them were too young for marriage, but she hadn't exactly wanted them to part ways like this, looking so uncomfortable and distressed. Especially not right before Christmas.

"I could make you both some tea," she said then, giving them a smile.

They were both quiet for so long that Renee almost turned away to go to the kitchen.

"What kind of tea?" Karyn finally asked.

"Lemon. Cinnamon. Orange spice. Regular and raspberry." Renee rattled off the choices. A couple of the men drank tea when they had a cold and Renee had a fondness for the brew, too, so she kept a variety of tea bags on hand.

"I'd like some lemon flavored," Karyn said as she glanced over at Eric. "If it's not too much trouble."

"No trouble at all," Renee said as she stood by the

door and slipped out of her boots. She walked over to the fireplace in her stockinged feet and added a piece of wood to the embers burning there. "I'll just get this going and then put some water on to boil in the kitchen."

The fire flared as it heated up.

"I could help you with that," Karyn said as she stood.

Renee figured the girl was searching for an excuse to leave for a bit and so she nodded.

A door opened at the end of the hall and Renee wondered which of the ranch hands had gotten up early. They clung to every moment of sleep they could get when it was cold outside, unless, of course, they had cows that were calving or fences that needed emergency fixes. Then they were up at odd hours all night and day.

Renee walked back to the door and was bending down to put on her boots when she saw someone walk into the room from the hallway. She looked up and saw Rusty.

The man had on a denim shirt and denim jeans. He looked ready for work even though his arm was still in a sling. He was fresh-shaven and his jet-black hair was neatly combed.

It was his eyes that drew her, though. He'd glanced around the room as if something was wrong and he needed to identify it before he moved farther into the area. She supposed it was a leftover from his military days, but it made her wonder if he could smell the conflict brewing between the two young people.

She had only a second to wonder before she knew

she was wrong about part of it, at least. The conflict wasn't between the young people.

Eric stood up, lifted the beige duffel until it was over his head and then threw it back to the floor. "What business do you have going into the barn out there?"

He looked enraged enough to spit at his brother, but Rusty didn't move a muscle to step out of his way.

"I didn't think anyone was using the buildings anymore," Rusty finally said, his voice mild. "Is that where you've been staying since you lied to the Morgans and said you had a job someplace?"

"I do have a job," Eric protested, sullen now. "Not that it's—"

Rusty held up his hand. "I know. It's none of my business."

"Well, it's not," Eric insisted, sitting back down on the sofa and folding his arms defiantly. "You haven't even been around for eight years and now you come back like you own the place."

Renee expected Rusty to remind his brother that neither of them owned their father's old ranch. She was going to try to catch his eye so she could head him away from the logical response, but she didn't have a chance.

"I know," Rusty said gently instead and Renee could hear the love in his voice. "I'm sorry for not coming back, but I thought it was best at the time."

Rusty walked over to the sofa and sat down. He left enough room between him and his brother so the boy didn't need to feel trapped. Neither said anything more, but Renee could feel the battling emotions coming from them.

She turned to Karyn. "Let's go get the tea."

The girl nodded, her gratitude obvious, and Renee finished putting her boots on. She gave one last look at Rusty and his brother before she left. It was long enough to see they were starting to talk, their voices low so no one else could hear.

Father, give Rusty the wisdom to know what to say, she prayed quickly before opening the door. The brothers needed each other. She only hoped they knew it.

Rusty didn't pay any attention to the door closing. He hadn't known Eric had this kind of pent-up anger toward him, but he wasn't going to add to it now. He knew his father wasn't an easy man to tolerate, but he'd always figured Eric had done better with the old man than he had. Maybe he'd only wanted to think that because it eased his conscience about leaving.

"What can I do to make it up to you?" Rusty asked finally when Eric had been silent for a bit. "We're brothers. I'm sorry."

Eric just shook his head.

Rusty put his left hand on his brother's back, hoping to show how much he cared. Eric flinched but Rusty knew it wasn't because of the teen's attitude toward him.

"Let me see your back," Rusty said quietly, hoping his suspicions were wrong. "No one's in the room. You can show me."

The panic on Eric's face confirmed Rusty's fears.

"I don't need to show you anything," Eric said, trying for belligerence, but sounding more afraid than anything.

"If someone has hurt you, I want to know," Rusty said.

"It's none of your—"

This time Rusty didn't let him finish. "Until you're eighteen, it is my business. I'm your guardian. I suppose if I called the sheriff and demanded he come out here, he would make sure I saw the skin on your back."

Eric looked shocked that such a thing could happen. Rusty wasn't sure it could, but he kept his eyes steady and firm.

Finally, Eric stood up and lifted the back of his shirt.

Rusty whistled silently. There were whiplash marks, some fresh and many that were old. "Who did this to you?"

"Our father," Eric said, spitting out the words.

Rusty closed his eyes in regret.

"He's been dead for four months," Rusty said then, realizing there was more to what happened. "He can't have done the new ones."

Eric didn't say anything.

"Answer me," Rusty commanded.

"I can't," Eric whispered. "If I tell, he'll kill us both."

"I'm not that easy to kill," Rusty said.

Eric tucked the back of his shirt into his jeans and sat down on the sofa again. He was silent for a while and Rusty let him rest. Whatever his brother had done, Rusty was at least partially responsible. He'd thought their phone calls were enough. He should have gone home to visit on his leaves from the army. His father would have hated it, but maybe the old man would have taken some of his anger out on Rusty instead of his brother.

"What were you doing up in the hayloft?" Rusty finally asked. "You had to be there to see my duffel."

"I was looking around," Eric said.

"You were getting the barn ready to hide stolen cattle, weren't you?" Rusty guessed. "I can't think of any other reason you'd be up there with those leftover hay bales. I'd guess there are enough to keep a herd of thirty cattle for a week or so. Sparse feedings, but it would work. And the water would be in the trough—no problem there. I wondered why the barn seemed in better shape than the house."

"Dad always did take care of the barn more than the house," Eric said, his voice sounding flat and defeated.

"Why'd you get involved in stealing cattle?" Rusty asked then. The Eric he remembered had been a nine-year-old boy, more interested in fishing than crime. And to listen to him talk about his enraged sense of justice over what had happened to their family in losing everything, he found it strange his brother would be willing to rob other ranch families.

"I didn't get involved," Eric said, his voice low. "I mean, I will be with the new shipment. But it wasn't my idea. I was staying in my old room at the house—" He looked up at Rusty defiantly. "The corporation that bought the place wasn't even around. No one's even seen them. It was still my room. But one day when I was there, this man came by. He tried chasing me off, but I'd just been out to the barn and seen the strange cattle penned up there. I made the mistake of telling him I knew what he was doing. He made me mad because—" Eric stopped and swallowed.

"Anyway, he threatened to kill me if I said anything. When I told him to try it, he said he'd kill Karyn after he did me in."

Eric sat quiet for a minute. "I couldn't risk it."

Rusty put his hand on his brother's arm. "We'll have to go to the sheriff with this, you know."

"We can't." Eric stood up, his whole body showing his panic. "The man will kill all of us for sure if we bring the law into this."

"I'll tell the sheriff we need a safe place for you and Karyn to stay," Rusty assured him as he rose, as well. "You'll need to tell us who this man is, though."

Eric shook his head.

Rusty looked down at the floor and saw his duffel. "Is that why you brought this back here? So he wouldn't know I'd been there, too?"

Eric nodded. "You only just got back. I didn't want—"

Rusty stepped a little closer and gave his brother a quick hug. "Don't worry about me. I plan to be around for a while."

The door to the bunkhouse opened again. Renee and Karyn were not using the cart this time, but each carried a dish. Snow was mixed in their hair and their noses were red. But they were safe and Rusty felt another jolt of sympathy with his brother. A man liked to protect the woman he loved, no matter what kind of laws people were breaking around them.

The ranch hands were coming down the hall, too.

Rusty turned to his brother. "Where have you been staying? Not in your old room, I hope."

Eric shook his head. "I did go out there this morning. But I've been staying in the barn at Karyn's place. Her parents don't know. She has an old diesel pickup she can drive if she wants. She doesn't like to drive it, but I do. The thing is like a tank and goes through snow drifts like you wouldn't believe. After I went to our old place, I swung by and got Karyn. I don't intend to have her out of my sight until that man—until he finishes with his cattle."

"We'll find a place where you can be protected," Rusty assured his brother. He didn't even want to get into all the other laws his brother was breaking by staying in an older couple's barn uninvited and using their pickup without their knowledge.

By that time, the ranch hands were all seated around the table. Karyn was passing around plates and bowls and silverware. Renee had just come back from the kitchen with four big thermos bottles, likely filled with coffee and tea, and a large pitcher of milk.

"Oatmeal with raisins and cinnamon rolls," Renee announced as she put the last thermos on the table. "Extra butter for the rolls and bananas to slice into the oatmeal if you want."

"Where's Tessie?" one of the ranch hands asked as he looked around the table.

"With my father," Renee said. "Likely playing checkers with him."

That seemed to satisfy the ranch hand. "She's good at them checkers."

Rusty let the warmth of the morning settle into his bones. The fire was giving off good heat and the mood around the table was friendly. He had people sitting here whom he wanted to protect.

Renee led the prayer before they ate, and Rusty joined in. He wasn't sure what his official relationship was with God, but he found he liked being surrounded by the faithful.

He didn't realize until the cinnamon rolls were passed for a second time that he wouldn't have all of this much longer. Somewhere inside his heart, he had started to hope for a life with Renee and Tessie. Oh, he had figured he'd need to work on the ranch as foreman for a year or so to prove they could trust him, but he was happy to do that. A woman like Renee deserved to be courted long and well.

But when Rusty talked to the sheriff, and he had no choice but to do so, all of his plans would be dashed. While a court might find his brother less guilty than charged when it came to rustling, people would suspect there was more to the story than Eric was telling.

Ranchers did not forgive cattle rustling. And this man Eric spoke of wasn't even named. Which meant the Calhoun brothers would shoulder the guilt in their neighbor's eyes.

Renee would never marry a man she thought might be a criminal. No matter what the people of Dry Creek said to their faces, he'd guess some would always believe he and Eric had known that rustlers were using their old barn. Others would believe there was no one else involved and that it was just the two of them. In the eyes of some, the Calhouns would even have motive—trying to put other ranchers out of business because they had lost their own place.

Almost all of the people around here would say it was no wonder the brothers ended up the way they had. They had not been raised in a proper home and their only influence was a mean-spirited father.

Rusty knew in his heart Renee was lost to him even if he never had the nerve to ask her to marry him. The suspicion would destroy any feelings she might have for him.

The second cinnamon roll on his plate didn't interest him any longer. The only hope they had, he finally concluded, was to find the man Eric refused to name. Rusty was going to have to let the sheriff set him up to go into the prison tomorrow. He'd do his best to get Renee's ex-husband to talk about anyone he knew in this area that he suspected of rustling. The rumors the sheriff would spread hardly mattered now; they were true enough and people would find out before long anyway.

Rusty looked across the table at his brother. The first thing was to call the sheriff and find a place to keep Eric safe. Then he'd make arrangements for the sheriff to attach a microphone to him.

Renee stood up and started collecting the empty pans. Rusty figured he had one more day before she knew everything. Maybe two. He intended to make the most of them.

Chapter Nine

Renee watched the blizzard through the windows in the Elkton house kitchen and knew when the snow stopped falling late that morning. A thin pile of flakes sat at the bottom of each window frame, frost swirling up farther on the glass. Minutes after the snow stopped, the clouds parted and sunlight broke through.

"I think we'll be able to go to Deer Lodge tomorrow," Renee said as she glanced over at Rusty. They were standing at the island counter in the middle of the kitchen and had been for the past ten minutes. The oven was preheating and she'd mixed up two batches of gingerbread dough several hours earlier. Rusty was examining the cookie cutters Mrs. Elkton had invited them to use. The rolling pin was sitting on the counter next to the dish of raisins to be used for eyes, and she had a sifter filled with flour ready to sprinkle on the marble countertop.

"So this is how you make gingerbread men," Rusty said, a note of awe in his voice. "I always thought people whittled them by hand with knives or something."

"Haven't you ever made cookies before?" Renee

asked as she set a small bowl of dried cherries by their work area.

"Not like this," Rusty said with a grin.

She was making her final check of what they needed, but spared him a smile. They'd use the cherry pieces for lips. She'd put an apron on, but she was none too sure she hadn't gotten some dough on her face. She wondered if they needed to put out walnut pieces for noses. Or maybe she could use the black jelly beans she'd purchased.

She was glad to see Rusty relaxed again. He'd rolled the sleeve of his denim shirt up to his elbow on one side and tucked a dish towel into his belt. He wouldn't be able to roll the dough with one arm in a sling, but he would have fun cutting out the gingerbread men.

She'd been worried about him.

After breakfast, he'd taken the bunkhouse phone into his room to make some calls. Eric had gone with him and the brothers hadn't come back for a half hour. By that time she and Karyn had finished washing the breakfast dishes and set the beef stew cooking for the noon meal.

"It's too bad Eric and Karyn couldn't join us," Renee remarked cautiously. Voicing general support was one thing, but she didn't want to pry. She knew Eric was upset and could only hope there had been some reconciliation.

"They're fine at that card table they set up in the bunkhouse." Rusty didn't meet her eyes. "They both have some homework they need to finish. The teacher is giving them extra time, but they'll be docked if they don't finish it before school starts again in January."

Renee nodded. "Their parents and teachers should make sure they have their homework done before they let them do anything together after school. That would help."

"I plan to do that," Rusty agreed. "If Eric and I ever get back into a normal life with each other again. I always thought he was telling me the truth on the phone."

Renee waited for him to say something more, but he didn't. She knew things weren't going well with the brothers. And as the younger Calhoun was fond of saying, it wasn't any of her business, but that didn't stop her from caring.

"Maybe after Christmas," Renee added when Rusty said nothing else. "You might find a house around here to rent, or maybe something in Miles City. It would be good if Eric could finish high school here. People always say that's important."

"No sense in switching in the middle of a year," Rusty agreed. "Especially the senior year. But I'll need to find a job if we plan to stay."

Renee finished rolling out their first circle of gingerbread dough and Rusty started to cut it into little men.

"There's an opening here on the ranch for a foreman," Renee said. She wasn't totally sure how she'd feel about that, but she couldn't hold back a man who needed work. Jobs were scarce.

"I heard," he said. "Pete told me."

"Oh." Renee might not have been sure about telling him the position existed, but she knew for sure she didn't like it that he knew and hadn't mentioned it to her. It made no sense. She'd like to think they were strong enough friends to confide a job consideration.

Then she realized he probably hadn't said anything about the job because he didn't plan to apply. She supposed this area wasn't very exciting to someone who had been away for so long.

They were both quiet for a while and then she heard a car horn.

"Oh, that'll be Tessie." Renee walked over to the sink to rinse her hands. She didn't want to add that stickiness to the doorknob. "My father phoned a while back and said the road from their place had been plowed."

"Let me check first," Rusty said as he almost ran to the door.

Dog barked before she managed to get to the door.

By that time, Rusty had already peeked out the crack as he slowly opened the door.

Tessie flew into her arms when the door was fully open, snow and blond hair flying every which way. Renee smiled down at her daughter. It was good to see her happy.

Renee looked up then at her father. "Thank you for giving her such a wonderful time."

"Tessie always does my heart good," he said in return. "But I better get back. Gracie wants me to take her to the café in Dry Creek for lunch and she wants to avoid the twelve o'clock crowd. You know her—you get six people in the whole place and she thinks something is wrong because people aren't staying home anymore."

Her father turned to walk back to his pickup. Renee noticed he stopped to pat Dog's head before he climbed in.

Renee closed the door and they all headed to the kitchen.

She tied a dish towel around her daughter's waist. "Wash up, now, before you start to help."

Tessie got the step stool she needed to reach the kitchen sink.

"Rinse twice and use soap," Renee instructed and then thought a moment. "Make that three rinses, since I'm sure you gave Dog a pat or two before you came to the door."

Tessie nodded her head and scrubbed her fingers. "Nice doggy."

Renee looked up to see Rusty studying her daughter.

"They're easier at that age," he said as he turned to her. "They do what they're told. Don't go off getting into trouble and not even telling you about it. They don't borrow cars from strangers and sleep in their girlfriend's barn."

"I think they're a challenge at any age," Renee said and then ventured further. "Did you resolve your trouble with Eric?"

Rusty nodded. "I'll tell you about it later. But I'm going to wear a wire tomorrow when we see—" He suddenly stopped and looked over to where Tessie stood on the stool leaning over the sink. "Well, I'll be wearing a microphone. That's all."

"Is that dangerous?" Renee asked.

"It'll be okay," Rusty said as he bent his head and concentrated on cutting out gingerbread men.

Within minutes, Tessie came over.

"This cookie cutter is bent," Rusty complained as he lifted one up and examined it. "My men don't have heads. They have mushrooms sticking out of their necks. Huge, fat mushrooms."

Tessie giggled.

"Here, you use them," Rusty said as he gave the cutters to the girl.

She took them with delight.

"You can help me pick out lips," Renee said as she moved the bowl of dried cherries so it was between them. "All I find are frowns."

"We want kisses," Tessie exclaimed as she pressed the cutter down into the thick layer of cookie dough. "And buttons for their bellies."

They were late for lunch because the gingerbread men were still baking. Karyn agreed to set the table. The stew was already in a large slow cooker, so she would just set that on the table and take the lid off.

Tessie didn't mention princes or castles once while she was making her gingerbread men, and Renee was hopeful she might be ready to give up her fantasies.

Something about the day marked it as different, though. The tree lights were on in the living room. Renee had cut twenty red ribbons to use as hangers for the gingerbread men on the tree.

Tessie had decorated one gingerbread man and called it Rusty. Then she decorated one that was supposed to be a woman named Renee. Last, she made a girl for herself.

Then she frowned and looked up at her mother. "Do I make one for Daddy, too?"

Renee wished she knew. "If you want."

Tessie seemed to consider it before nodding. "I'll make one to take when we go see him. He probably doesn't have Christmas in his castle."

"No, he probably doesn't," Renee agreed softly.

Renee almost sighed. When she'd bought the pine tree in Miles City and brought it home to decorate, she had been determined that she and her daughter would have one of those storybook holidays this year. The Christmas tree. The turkey. The presents.

Now she wondered if this Christmas wouldn't just break their hearts. Tessie would likely lose her father and her prince. Renee would lose the green shoots of love that had started to appear in her heart. She was going to have to tear them out.

As she'd made cookies today, she realized that there was no reason for Rusty to refuse to talk about his conflict with his brother unless it was related to the cattle thefts in some way. Eric wore his guilt visibly and had muttered something to Karyn about stolen cattle that she hadn't been able to figure out but had confided to Renee.

The man with the cookie cutter in his hand now was too good to be true and she knew it.

Rusty put on the coat Renee had lent him and walked back to the bunkhouse at three o'clock in the afternoon. He kept an eye on the few trees that ran along the edge of the corrals and the openings into the barn. He didn't think the man in the orange parka would know to look for him or Eric at the Elkton ranch, but he wasn't taking any chances. It reassured him somewhat that Dog was on patrol—he wouldn't tolerate a stranger snooping around.

The sheriff had been in Miles City for a dentist appointment and was coming to the bunkhouse as soon as he could get there, he said. The lawman had put in a request for the county to run the snowplow down the gravel road to the Elkton ranch so he could talk to Eric. Of course, Sheriff Wall wanted to convince Rusty's brother to reveal the man he was shielding. Rusty doubted the lawman would have any better success getting Eric to talk than he had. But it wouldn't hurt to have the sheriff assure the boy once again he and Karyn would be safe if he told what he knew.

Dog slipped around the side of the barn and loped over.

Rusty squatted down in the snow so he could rub the dog's ears. It was a habit he and Dog had formed when the animal was a puppy.

"Good Dog," Rusty assured his pet. They'd both stopped to visit Annie several times already today. The mare was comfortable in the Elkton barn and she didn't lack for company. He noticed one of the ranch hands had given her some oats midmorning.

He stood up and gestured for Dog to continue on patrol. Then Rusty finished walking through the snow to the bunkhouse. He stomped along the walkway when he arrived, hoping to loosen the snow that was packed on the soles of his boots.

The sheriff's pickup was driving down the lane before Rusty opened the door to the bunkhouse. He could not see the vehicle, but he could hear it, and the gray smoke of the exhaust told him the pickup was there.

Rusty could still smell the stew from noon as he stood inside the door. The ranch hands were all out in the barn and corrals. The card table that he had set up for Eric and Karyn so they could do their homework was empty. For a moment, Rusty feared his brother had managed to run away from the Elkton ranch after all.

But then he heard a giggle coming from the room at the end of the hall.

He made enough noise walking down there in his boots that he figured he'd given the two teenagers ample notice he was coming.

Eric was the first one to put his head around the door and say "Huh?"

Karyn followed seconds after, smoothing down her hair and trying to look serious. "Hello, Mr. Calhoun."

Rusty had to admit that put him off his stride. He had always been addressed by his first name or his rank in the service. His father had been the one to answer to Mr. Calhoun.

Rusty figured a responsible parent would have something wise to say to the two young people at a time like this. He looked over their clothing, though, and figured they hadn't been breaking too many rules. And if a kiss or two would soften his stubborn brother into cooperating with the authorities, it was okay with him.

"Sheriff's coming," Rusty said as he turned and walked back to the main room in the bunkhouse.

"Oh."

Rusty heard the girl behind him gasp in alarm.

"I'm not going to tell him anything," Eric said, his voice filled with resolve. "He can come, but I'll just sit there and stare at him."

"The sheriff wants to help you."

Eric snorted. "He's an old man. Sheriff Wall wouldn't know how to find his way out of a paper bag in the dark."

Rusty turned around to face his brother. "Keep a civil tongue in your head."

"I'm just saying what Dad used to say." Eric defended himself. "He didn't think much of the sheriff."

Rusty shook his head. "I hope you don't take our father as an example of the way you want to live your life."

Eric was silent at that.

Rusty heard a slight bark and recognized it as Dog's. "The lawman will be here soon."

The bunkhouse phone rang and Rusty stepped over to answer it. There was a pen and message pad beside the phone and all the calls were recorded there. "Hello?"

"I thought Karyn might want to come over here and have a cup of hot cider and a cookie with Tessie and me," Renee said.

"I'll let her know," Rusty replied.

After saying goodbye, he gave Karyn the message. The teenager smiled in relief and said that sounded good to her. Then she stood on her tiptoes and gave Eric a kiss on the cheek.

The gesture made Rusty blink a couple of times. He and his brother hadn't known much love in their lives. He couldn't fault Eric in his choice of a girlfriend; he could only hope their affection for each other would last long enough for them to get an education before they thought of marriage.

The sheriff knocked on the bunkhouse door and Karyn let him in as she slipped out, her coat and multiple scarves pulled snugly around her.

"Come have a seat." Rusty invited the lawman over

to the couch area. Then he stopped and put another piece of wood on the fire. "We might as well be comfortable. Like something to drink?"

Renee kept large thermoses of coffee on a buffet by the window, along with creamer and sugar. The ranch hands told him that was something she had added to her duties. Most afternoons she also left a snack there for any of the men who wanted to come inside for a break. None of the men said it outright, but Rusty could tell they were very fond of Renee and Tessie.

The sheriff sat down. "I'm fine, but thanks for the offer."

"Eric," Rusty said as he sat down on the sofa opposite the lawman. His brother reluctantly sat on the couch a foot or so from Rusty.

They were all silent for a moment. All Rusty heard was the crackle of the fire as the flames covered the wood he'd added. He glanced toward the windows on the opposite wall of the bunkhouse and confirmed no snow was blowing. He was almost ready to count the planks in the flooring when the sheriff finally started his conversation with Eric.

"I understand you have been in contact with one of the rustlers," the lawman said. "Care to tell me more about him?"

"Not particularly," Eric said, his voice indifferent.

Rusty held down his frustration with his brother. He could understand the teenager was scared, but he didn't have to antagonize anyone.

Sheriff Wall shrugged. "Your choice. I can pull you in for questioning if you want."

Eric's face went white. "I'd be dead by morning. I have strict instructions not to talk to the law."

"I see," the sheriff said as he nodded. "I could put you in a safe house."

"Same thing," Eric said. "This man says he has contacts. I don't know who they are and I don't want to know."

The sheriff leaned back into the cushions on the sofa and waited a bit. "He almost killed your brother, you know? I would think you'd want to do something about that."

"I am doing something," Eric said as he stood up. "I'm trying to keep him alive."

With that, Eric walked down the hall and into the bedroom he'd been given permission to use. Then he slammed the door, the echo reverberating in the bunkhouse.

"I'm sorry," Rusty said when the noise had subsided.

"Not your fault," the sheriff said as he stood up. "Now, let's get the microphone set up for your big day tomorrow." He stopped. "And before I forget, I have Renee's papers for her. The lawyer gave them to me this morning and asked me to pass them on to her. The guy has his office in the same building as my dentist."

"That saves us a stop in the morning," Rusty said as he stood up.

"I've already left a message for my contact at the prison. He'll know how to get the rumor started that you're running on the wrong side of the law."

"I appreciate it," Rusty said as he walked over to the dining table. "I'm going to sit down so I can loosen my sling. That way it'll be easier to get a small microphone hidden in there."

The sheriff bent down to study Rusty's sling before sliding a clip-on recording device into the fabric at his elbow. "You bring this back to me when you're done and we'll see what we have."

Rusty nodded. "And you want me to mention the rustling and see if he gives up any names of others doing the same kind of thieving."

"Pretty much," the sheriff agreed. "It's only a hunch that he knows anything. If he doesn't, we'll have to start over."

"With Eric?" Rusty asked.

The sheriff nodded. "I'm trying this way first, but if we don't find anything useful, I'll have to bring Eric in. He'll get a lawyer and he'll be advised not to talk, but he might want to cut a deal for himself. He's guilty of obstruction of justice if he doesn't tell us what he knows."

"He's only seventeen."

"That's why I'm giving him another couple of days to come to his senses. I figure he has tomorrow, when you go the prison, and then the next day is Christmas Eve. I can't pull someone from the pageant at the last minute. At least, not someone who has a major role. The ranch hands won't let him out of their sight between now and then, anyway."

Everyone concerned had decided the best safe place for Eric and Karyn was at the ranch. The hands were sharp enough to keep the two teenagers there.

Rusty nodded. "I'll do my best to get you what you need to know."

"Eric is right about one thing," the sheriff said. "Whoever is behind this rustling isn't somebody to be messed with. Take care of yourself."

The sheriff turned to leave. "Oh, and you might want to put this back in your boot." He reached into his pocket and drew out the knife they had taken in the hospital. "You'll need to give it up when you go into the prison, but you'll have it with you for the rest of the trip."

"Thanks," Rusty said as he pocketed the knife.

When the sheriff left, he sat back down on the couch and stared into the fire. He and his brother were going to have a hard time if Eric refused to name the mystery man was who was using their barn.

Rusty couldn't imagine the unknown man was any of the other ranchers around here. The drought had already taken their profits for the past few years. Stealing cattle could put most of these ranches out of business.

Ranching was a hard business, but like his brother, Rusty still had strong ties to the land that had belonged to his family for three generations. He didn't suppose there was much hope of it happening, but after Christmas he intended to find out what corporation had bought his family's ranch and see if he could buy it back. He had a down payment—not much, but maybe enough to tempt a group that wasn't using the place anyway.

His father used to have a friend at the bank in Havre. Rusty decided that maybe he'd go in and talk to the man. Otis something was his name, and he talked with a lisp. His father had had so few friends that Rusty remembered the tall, skinny man from a visit he'd made

with his father to the bank one spring day. His father
had needed money for seed and Otis was the one who
approved the loan. He even added a line of credit, saying it was because he was his father's friend.

Rusty reminded himself that it was that loan, or
one like it, that the bank had used to foreclose on the
ranch. They denied receiving the payment his father
said he'd made.

It was so unlike his father to lie that Rusty had always believed he'd made that payment. But now he
wondered if his father and not the bank had been cheat-
ing. His father had changed over the years, and not for
the better. Maybe he hadn't made the payment.

Rusty stood as he reflected again that ranching was
a difficult way to make a living. But then, he told himself, his most recent job involved getting shot at on a
regular basis. Maybe the Calhouns were not meant for
desk jobs.

He looked over at the thermoses on the buffet again.
Renee wasn't a routine person, either. She put everything she had into what she was doing. He wondered
how their visit to the prison would go tomorrow. He
had been thinking so much about how to get her ex-
husband to talk about rustling that he had almost forgotten that the main thing the man needed to do was
talk to his daughter.

He shook his head. He couldn't believe any man
would give up a wife like Renee and a daughter like
Tessie. Some men were just fools. He only hoped that
this fool would help bring down another crook.

Chapter Ten

Renee had set her alarm for six o'clock in the morning and it rang loudly in her ear. The bedroom was dark and she looked over at the illuminated hands on the clock to be sure it was indeed that time.

She was hoping for a reprieve, but there was none to be found.

"Tessie." She reached over to wake her daughter. The girl was practically buried under blankets. She groaned as she turned over and then pulled the top blanket closer.

Neither of them was going to bounce out of bed this morning. Renee wondered if Rusty was moving any faster in the bunkhouse. He had suggested they get an early start and leave at a quarter to seven.

It had sounded like a good idea then, Renee told herself, since the drive over to Deer Lodge would take five or six hours.

Fortunately, Renee didn't have to worry about the bunkhouse today. Karyn was spending the night in the cook's quarters and had agreed to fill in for Renee today for all three meals, and Renee was grateful. Food was much more important to the ranch hands in winter than in summer—when cold seeped into their bones and their arthritis was painful, they liked a few extras with their meals, too. So they'd be happy. Karyn had promised to make buttermilk pancakes for them and heat the maple syrup the way they liked. She might even fry some of that smoked bacon Renee had bought recently.

"Mommy," Tessie finally muttered.

"Time to get up," Renee said as she pushed herself up with an elbow.

"Do I see Daddy today?"

Renee let herself fall back to the mattress. "Remember what we talked about last night?"

She could see Tessie nodding even in the gray light.

"Well, we're going to where Daddy lives now." Renee repeated the words from yesterday. "If you want to see him and talk to him, you can. If you want to see him but not talk to him, that's okay, too. If you want me to talk to him for you and bring a message out to the car, that's fine, too. You have three choices. You get to pick."

"I don't know."

Renee reached over and rubbed her daughter's back. She'd called the therapist in Billings and the woman had said Tessie was likely ready to speak with her father but shouldn't be forced. "You can think about it on the way over to Deer Lodge. You won't have to do anything you're not ready to do."

Tessie was silent for a moment.

"Will he remember me?" she finally asked, her voice a whisper.

"I'm sure he will," Renee assured her. Even her ex-husband could not be so cruel.

"Okay," Tessie said as she rolled over to the edge of the bed. "Is my prince going, too?"

"Yes, Rusty is going." Renee wasn't going to repeat her *there are no princes* words. Not with Tessie's worries. If the girl needed to trust her prince in order to face her father, Renee was going to keep her mouth shut about it. There would be time later to help her daughter face her fantasies. Today all Tessie needed to do was see the man whose genes she carried.

"I'll get up now," Tessie said.

"I'm glad," Renee said as she sat on the edge of the bed, too. "What do you want to wear today?"

Tessie smiled. "I want to show my daddy my angel wings. He doesn't know angels can fly away."

"I'm not sure—" Renee said, trying to think of the best answer. Her ex-husband wasn't the kind to coo over something like that. "They don't allow everything into the prison where your daddy is staying."

"They let angel wings everywhere," Tessie said as she spread her arms and walked out of the room.

Please, God, she prayed, *let that be true.*

The girl went into her room and put on her red sparkling dress and her angel wings.

Renee wondered if she should call the sheriff. The lawman would know if there was any chance of taking Tessie's angel wings into the visitors' room. Although when she thought about it, there was no metal on the wings. Cotton balls and gold glitter decorated the edge of them, but the rest was just cardboard painted white.

Given the festive glamour of Tessie's clothes, Renee

decided to wear her denim jeans and an old blue sweater. She didn't want her ex-husband to think this was a Christmas celebration of some kind and that they were hoping for a greeting-card moment.

By the time she had strapped Tessie into her booster seat and tucked the angel wings behind the driver's seat, Rusty was there and climbing into the passenger's side. They pulled out of the Elkton place at seven o'clock. It felt like five.

Renee had packed a thermos of coffee and another one of juice. She had bananas and apples for snacking. They were packing light, she thought, considering that Tessie had wanted to bring Dog with them.

As much as Renee would like to greet her ex-husband with a wolf at her side, she figured Dog wouldn't enjoy the trip. Besides, she wasn't sure that the animal wouldn't be banned as a weapon.

Truthfully, all she wanted was to slip in and get her ex-husband to sign the custody papers for Tessie and have him say a couple of insincere words to their daughter then let them leave in peace.

There had been some snow on the gravel roads when they left the Elkton ranch, but when they got to the freeway, it was clear. The road was still frozen and had a scraped look, but there wasn't any snow. As the sun rose, the day warmed. The sky was light blue and there was no frost on the windshield.

"You don't need us with you when you talk to my ex, do you?" Renee asked Rusty. She'd forgotten for a while there was more to this trip than just herself and Tessie.

"No, I think he'd talk better if we were alone,"

Rusty said. "Unless he refuses to talk to me without you there."

"I doubt that," Renee said. Her ex didn't value her opinion. "Unless of course he just wants to make things difficult for me."

It was silent for a moment.

"I don't suppose you'd like to tell me about him," Rusty finally said. "Anything that might help me get him to talk?"

"Like what?"

"What kind of sports he likes, political hot buttons, hobbies?" Rusty said. "Something that will help me put him at ease. Make him feel he's talking to a buddy. Maybe his first name. I notice you never use it."

"His name is Denny," Renee said curtly. "And I don't use his name because—well, I just don't. He's my ex and that's all. Except for being Tessie's daddy."

"Well, that's a start."

Renee noticed the tension in her hands as she gripped the wheel. Talking about her ex-husband made her nervous.

"He also liked football," Renee continued, forcing herself to go on. "I don't know if he still does. He used to have the car radio tuned to country music—when we had a radio that worked, anyway. He liked to chew gum. Spearmint, mostly."

"Okay," Rusty nodded. "Regular kind of guy."

"If you call robbing banks regular," Renee said with some punch behind her words.

"Of course not," Rusty answered back testily. "I'm not soft on crime, either, just in case you are wondering. I don't approve of what my brother has done so far.

And I certainly want the man who's threatening him caught and sent to jail."

Tessie hiccuped in the backseat and that was all Renee needed. Her daughter did that when she started getting scared. Renee didn't know what caused it physically—maybe a lack of air—but she needed to turn this around. She might not like this conversation, but she hated that Tessie might be worried.

"I'm sorry," Rusty said then, his voice low and distressed. "That was uncalled for—"

Renee was speechless. The other times Tessie had hiccuped like that, she and her ex-husband had been squabbling. She had always been the one to stop it. To apologize. To accept the blame. To promise never to do it again.

"I—" She started. Maybe she would learn something about herself by talking about her past. "It's my fault, too."

"It's a hard day for us all," Rusty agreed. "We'll just call it even."

Renee spared a quick glance over to make sure he looked sincere. He did.

"I usually—" She turned her eyes back to the road. It was only in the past year that she had done any of this kind of thinking. "Have you been talking with Pastor Curtis?"

"No." He shook his head. "My chaplain."

"Aah," she said.

He smiled then. "I used to apologize before I knew it was good for the soul, too. I was born knowing I made mistakes. My mother reminded me."

Renee considered that. "There's a difference between knowing you've made a mistake and openly apologizing for it."

Rusty nodded. "There's a difference between a small mistake and a large one, too. Some things are too big for apologies."

His voice was quiet and Renee could almost feel the pain of his words. She didn't know what he meant, though.

"Jesus didn't think so," she finally said. "He forgave everything."

"Jesus never made a mistake that got his whole platoon killed," Rusty said, and the words hung in the air between them. "He never left his brother in the care of an abusive old man. He never disappointed his mother so badly she left."

The bitterness of his grief was almost too much.

"I'm so sorry," she said.

Rusty gave a curt nod. "I'm working through it. That chaplain I know is one persistent guy."

"Good," she said softly. "That's good."

They passed the next hour in silence, but Renee decided the quiet was important for both of them. She certainly had things to sort through. The anger she felt for her ex-husband—that would be Denny, she made a point of saying to herself—had not lessened. When had she stopped using his name, as though he was less of a person?

She looked in her rearview mirror. Tessie was sleeping in her booster seat, the tip of her wing showing by her black shoe and her red dress sparkling in the sun that came in the side window. Renee wondered if her feelings toward Denny had made Tessie more afraid of the man. Maybe she had been part of the reason for her daughter's fantasies. She didn't remember Denny ever showing affection to their daughter, but maybe Tessie had tapped into her mother's rage and built her conflicted fantasies from that. Renee knew she smiled sometimes when the subject of Tessie's father came up even though she was seething inside.

No, Renee told herself suddenly, she wasn't going to be the fall guy in this. Any man who hit his child did not have the right to be forgiven.

She looked over at Rusty. She had told him nothing was unforgivable. Had she been wrong? She had no inclination to absolve her ex-husband. Rusty seemed tormented by as many questions as she was.

Rusty could see the Deer Lodge prison from a distance as they turned off the freeway next to the small town. A squared-off two-story building in a light gray color with rows of windows on all sides squatted on the open land like the cement box it was. The dirt road that went to the main gate was plowed and had no snow on it. The ground was frozen. A wire fence surrounded everything and tall spotlights rose in even spaces, their shining metal heads pointing down at the prison grounds.

They had stopped to buy gas for the pickup an hour earlier and Rusty had gone inside the station and bought an assortment of candy bars and lots of spearmint gum. He didn't feel any more prepared to meet Denny Hampton than he had been yesterday. He had never laid eyes on the man and already he despised him. If he let that show, though, all chance of getting him to talk would be gone.

Renee drove through the gate into the parking area for visitors. After she parked, she turned to Rusty.

"Are we doing the right thing?" she asked.

He had been reaching for the handle to open his door, but he stopped and looked at her. "Nervous?"

She nodded.

"I can take the custody papers in for you if you want," Rusty offered.

She shook her head. "I don't think he'd sign them. I'm not even sure he'll sign them if I give them to him, but I'm sure he won't sign for anyone else. He'll want to make me suffer first by pretending he won't sign. Trying to get me to beg. Having some fun at my expense."

"Sounds like a prince of a guy," Rusty said, forgetting Tessie was in the backseat.

"No, you're the prince," Tessie said, leaning toward the front seat. "Not my daddy."

Rusty turned around. "Do you still want to see your father?"

"Remember you have three choices," Renee added as she looked at her daughter.

The girl looked serious.

"I want to see my daddy myself," Tessie finally said, nothing of fairy-tale endings in her voice. She looked as if she knew it wouldn't be pleasant. But she needed to face the man.

Rusty decided not to make them look like a family when they left the pickup. It would be easier for all that way, he thought. But when the sidewalk to the entrance was slick, he gave one arm to Renee to hold on to. He'd already picked up Tessie when she'd wobbled in the wind with her wings.

They made an odd sight, he was sure, but he suddenly wished he had a picture of them making their way to those old metal doors anyway.

It wasn't until they opened the doors to go inside that Rusty made a decision. The tension in all of them was out of control.

"Do you think there's someplace where we can pray?" he asked Renee. "Well, more you praying and me agreeing, but you know what I mean."

She smiled up at him. "I'd like to find a quiet room. I put our trip on the prayer chain at church yesterday. Telling people that we were looking for answers and going to talk to my ex-husband."

Rusty felt a moment's unease. "Did you mention me? That I was looking for these answers, too?"

Renee nodded. "I guess. I mean, I didn't say much. Just that the three of us were going and then the answers bit."

"Who gets the prayer requests?" Rusty asked, telling himself he was worrying needlessly. The sheriff had mentioned that the rustlers might put pressure on Renee's ex-husband if he had some information they thought he might spill. The prayer requests probably only went to three old ladies who talked everything over while they had their tea.

"Everybody," Renee said with a shrug. "There's an internet loop. Anyone who wants can get the messages."

By that time, Renee had found a small waiting room that was empty. She led them all inside. The walls were painted a light mauve and the chairs were upholstered with an old navy vinyl. A bouquet of yellow plastic flowers sat on a scarred coffee table beside a stack of old magazines.

"I don't know how long this room will be ours," she said as she sat down on one of the chairs. "So we'll pray fast."

Rusty sat down, setting Tessie in her own chair. Then they all joined hands and bowed their heads.

Rusty nodded every time Renee asked for guidance or wisdom. He knew he didn't really qualify as someone who should pray since he wasn't sure about God's forgiveness yet, but the chaplain had encouraged him to act beyond what he believed when it came to prayer. The important thing, the man said, was that Rusty believed God was listening. Then he added that maybe that wasn't even necessary. Maybe it was nothing more than a man bringing his concerns to God and trusting Him to take care of them.

Everything in him that was protective rose up when Tessie asked Jesus to help her talk to her daddy. He even prayed for that one himself, telling God he would appreciate the girl's request being answered.

It wasn't long after they prayed that the three of them were standing in a hallway, waiting to be searched. The angel wings caused some eyebrows to rise and some lips to curve, but they were permitted. Then a guard escorted them into the large beige visitors' room. The inmates were able to sit at a table with a plastic window between them and their guests.

The sheriff had done a good job with his arrangements, because all three of them were scheduled to see Denny Hampton.

Rusty was surprised by his first view of the man. He was shorter than Rusty thought he would be. And he had red hair, or maybe it was dark auburn. The orange jumpsuit made his skin look green. His face was drawn and he squinted as he watched Rusty, Renee and Tessie walk over to the table.

Rusty had thought about putting Tessie down. She'd put her wings on her back and it blocked some of Rusty's vision. But the girl clung to him until he only tightened his hold on her.

"You couldn't wait, could you?" Denny snarled as he leaned back, looking from Renee to Rusty. He didn't even glance at Tessie.

"It's not what it looks like," Renee stammered.

"I doubt that," Denny said with a sneer on his face. "I'd guess it's a whole lot more than it looks like. What's the matter? Did you get a little lonely at night?"

"I spend my time with our daughter," Renee said, her voice gaining some strength as she sat down in front of the plastic window. "I brought you papers to sign so that Tessie is taken care of if something should happen."

Renee slipped the documents through the slit under the plastic.

Rusty took a position behind her, Tessie with an arm around Rusty's neck as she twisted around to look at her father, her wings flapping a little as she did. She had a gingerbread cookie in her hand.

Denny didn't even glance at the papers.

The man stared at Rusty instead. "Who's that you got with you?"

Rusty tightened his hold on Tessie. The girl was trembling.

"It's me, Daddy," she said, her voice shimmering with hope. "Your princess."

Denny Hampton started to laugh and it had a mean sound to it.

"I don't have a princess," he finally managed to say.

Rusty put his hand on Tessie's back as though he could shield her from the man.

"What you have is a daughter," Renee said then, her voice rising in volume until she was almost shouting. "So sign those papers."

Denny put back his head and grinned. "I see you finally got some spunk to you. It's about time."

Renee stood up then and, if it were possible, Rusty had no doubt she would have leaped over the partition separating her from her ex-husband.

"You're a vile, evil man!" she said through gritted teeth.

Denny looked taken back and a little afraid. Rusty noticed the prisoner looked over his shoulder at the guard in the back of the room, as though he needed reassurance.

"You can't talk to me that way," he said in protest, his voice drawn out until it became a whine. "I know people."

"Sign the papers and you can know all the pathetic people you want," Renee said, her voice cold and forceful. She sat back down in the chair. She clearly didn't believe him that he knew anyone who could hurt her.

"I don't have a pen," Denny said.

Rusty reached into his pocket and held out a ballpoint pen. He'd asked when he went through security if this was allowed in the visitors' room. The guard had approved it.

"You should read the thing first," Renee cautioned him. "It's a legal document."

"I don't need to read it," the man said, his voice flat. "I don't want anything more to do with the girl. Legal or otherwise."

"Don't say that," Renee said, gentler than she had been. "Someday you might—"

She stopped then and didn't say any more.

They were all silent for a moment, just looking at each other through the plastic partition.

Finally, Denny bent his head and put his signature on the document. Renee had already told Rusty that she was putting her father down as Tessie's backup guardian.

When the documents were dated and signed, Denny pushed them back. Renee grabbed them and put them in her purse.

"Thank you," she said to her ex-husband, her voice exhausted, but no longer as angry. "At least you did the decent thing for once."

With that, Renee stood up and added, "Someone else wants to talk to you."

Rusty gave Tessie to her mother. The girl looked frozen in shock. He had seen that same expression on young recruits in the army when their whole world changed.

He leaned over and whispered in the girl's ear, "It'll be all right. I promise."

She looked up him and nodded. Then the first tear rolled down her cheek.

Rusty watched as Renee and Tessie left the visitors' room. Then he reached into his sling and took out all the candy and gum he'd bought earlier. While he was doing that, he turned on the microphone.

He set the candy down on the ledge on his side of the plastic partition and settled into the chair.

"I've been expecting you," Denny said with a wide smile. "Had to get rid of the missus so we could talk."

Rusty was speechless, so he pushed the candy through the opening. Denny picked up a package of the gum and smiled.

"Thanks," he said.

"No problem," Rusty replied.

They both sat there while the man opened the package and pulled out a stick of gum. He slowly unwrapped it and put it in his mouth.

"My, that's fine," he said as he started to chew.

The man worked his jaw for a good minute before he was ready to talk again.

"You need to tell your brother to cool it," Denny finally said. "That's my message to you. He's making the man nervous and he doesn't want to do that. The man's afraid he'll identify him."

Rusty couldn't believe it would be this easy, but he leaned closer anyway so the microphone could pick up every word.

"Just who is my brother making nervous?"

Denny chuckled. "You know I can't say something like that in here. These walls have ears. Besides, as I understand it, you know more than I do. The Calhoun boys are in deep. Just keep your kid brother in line and you'll do fine."

Rusty was stunned. "What did you say?"

"That's right," Denny said with a wink. "Never admit anything."

Then the visiting time was over. Just like that. The guard came over and shut the partition. Denny stood up and shuffled back to the door to the rest of the prison.

Rusty walked out of the room in a daze. Was he that out of touch with his brother? They'd talked together for hours last night. Eric was candid about refusing to name his mystery man, but he had seemed straight about everything else. Was he lying?

As Rusty made his way down the hall, he saw Renee and Tessie waiting for him on a bench near the main door. Tessie was curled up on her mother's lap, her head bowed and her angel wings sticking out from her back awkwardly. She looked wounded and Rusty wished he'd never encouraged her to come.

Denny Hampton had filled them all with grief today. Making them question what they believed about those they loved.

Renee and Tessie looked up as Rusty approached. The girl squirmed off her mother's lap and ran to Rusty. He picked her up without question and her head rested against his shoulder.

Then he stood beside Renee, looking down at the haunted expression in her eyes. "We're going to be all right."

She gave him a slight smile. "So Tessie told me."

Together they walked out of the building.

"On the drive back," Renee said as they neared the

pickup, "we should rehearse your lines for the pageant. It's coming up tomorrow night."

Then she looked at her daughter in his arms. "Tessie can help."

Rusty felt the girl nod her head against his chest.

"My pleasure," Rusty said as he opened the back door on the pickup and strapped Tessie into her booster seat. She already looked better.

"I can use my wings," the girl murmured.

Renee was an expert at picking up the pieces and going on, Rusty told himself. He'd never admired a woman more. When he climbed into the passenger seat, she was already behind the wheel, but she looked over at him. The glance she gave him was grateful, but it promised a hint of something more lasting. He felt his breath lodge in his throat.

She was open to more between them, he could see that. But he couldn't say anything now because she might not be so very open once she heard the tape he'd just made. He had no choice but to give it to the sheriff. Denny Hampton hadn't just pointed a finger at Eric—he had said Rusty was involved, too. Renee would not like that.

"Do you have a crown for when you're king?" Tessie asked Rusty as her mother backed out of the parking space.

Rusty shook his head as he turned to face the girl. "We'll have to make one when we get home."

Tessie brightened at that.

Maybe everything would be all right, Rusty told

himself. Then he sighed. He just didn't believe it. But he wouldn't let his sense of foreboding spoil Tessie's enjoyment in getting ready for the pageant.

Chapter Eleven

The next morning, Renee hung the last of the ginger-bread men on their Christmas tree before going over to the bunkhouse. Tessie hadn't needed an alarm clock to wake up this morning. When Renee rolled over at six o'clock, she saw her daughter lying there, staring up at the ceiling.

"What's wrong?" Renee had asked softly.

"Does God see my daddy when he looks down from heaven?" the girl questioned.

Renee pulled her daughter close for a hug. "God sees everyone everywhere."

After a breakfast of oatmeal, Renee gave Tessie one of the broken gingerbread men to eat before she got ready to walk over to the bunkhouse. A plate of the gingerbread men stood on top of the refrigerator waiting for them to come home after the pageant tonight.

The sky was overcast and gray clouds were in the north when they stepped outside. There was no wind and the temperature was in the mid-forties.

They walked briskly, but hadn't bundled up as much as usual.

"Will Rusty be here?" Tessie asked just before they reached the bunkhouse door. "When we open our presents?"

Tessie had drawn her prince a picture of Dog, tied it with a bright red ribbon for Rusty and included a dog biscuit for his animal.

"We'll need to invite him." Renee said.

Earlier, she had wrapped some bacon around chestnuts and stuffed some mushrooms so she'd have a heartier appetizer in case Rusty did want to come. She hoped he would. He was beginning to feel like family to her, and Tessie obviously adored him.

When they went inside the bunkhouse, Tessie walked over to the card table that had been left by the fireplace and laid down the coloring books she'd brought with her. Renee took the box of crayons from her pocket and took it over to set by the books. She had offered to let Tessie bring her new princess coloring book, but the girl had shaken her head and brought her farm book with the horses instead.

Tessie hadn't spun any more fanciful tales about her father, not even this morning after she worried about God being able to see him. Renee wasn't sure if that meant Tessie was going to give up her fantasies or not. All she knew was that as Tessie's mother, she wasn't even ready to pray for the grace to forgive her daughter's father. He hadn't needed to be so cruel.

Breakfast was over at the bunkhouse when the sheriff arrived at nine o'clock. Renee opened the door for the lawman but it was clear he was there on business. He said only a brief hello before going to the back room to talk with Rusty and Eric.

Renee went about cleaning up the table, loading the dishes onto her cart and going over several times to admire the coloring Tessie had done.

Twenty minutes later, the sheriff walked down the hallway and let himself out. When she saw how grim his face was, Renee didn't even say goodbye to the lawman.

Moments later, Eric stomped out of the bunkhouse, stating that he had to go to Karyn's place and see about that donkey her parents had offered to loan to the pageant tonight.

Rusty must have followed close behind his brother, because he was standing at the end of the hall when Eric left. He had a look of weariness on his face.

"Trouble?" Renee asked as she walked over and stood beside him. She was almost finished putting the breakfast dishes in the cart and would then need to chop cabbage for the coleslaw for noon, but she had time to talk if he needed.

"Some days I've got nothing but trouble," Rusty said as he gave her a wry smile.

He hadn't shaved yet today and his stubble gave him a tough look. The defeated expression in his eyes didn't help, either.

"If I can help, let me know," she offered.

"I just don't know what to do," Rusty finally admitted.

Renee longed to lean in and hug the man.

Rusty flashed a look at her and then closed his eyes as though he was in pain.

"You never did say if my ex—if Denny—gave you

any good information for the sheriff," Renee finally said, keeping her voice low so Tessie couldn't hear.

Rusty opened his eyes then, searching hers for something.

"The news isn't good," he finally said. "From what the sheriff can see, anyway. Eric still won't identify the man he knows about. And Denny implied my brother and I are part of whatever is happening."

Renee was too stunned to speak.

"I suspect the word will get around that Eric and I are persons of interest in the cattle thefts," Rusty added. "I'm wondering if we should bow out of being in the pageant tonight. I wouldn't want us to detract from the kids."

"I'm sure Mrs. Hargrove would want you to play your parts," Renee said, numb herself. "People have had all kinds of reasons to pull out of the pageant in the past and she's always said we need to just go out there and tell the story of Jesus's birth."

"It's not always that easy," Rusty said.

"I know," Renee agreed.

They were silent for a moment, looking at each other warily.

"It would help if I knew you trusted me," he said then, so faintly she almost didn't hear him.

Renee already felt herself withdrawing. Even if she loved him, she wasn't willing to try to prop up another man as he slid into a life of crime.

"What does the sheriff say?" she asked.

Rusty's face went stiff. "He probably thinks my brother and I are guilty. And I suppose he plans to prove it."

"Oh," Renee said. "I'm sorry."

Rusty gave a curt nod and started to walk toward the door. When he got there, he turned. "Do you happen to know of anyone around here who has an orange parka?"

Renee shrugged. "One of the high school girls, Leslie, has a big parka with an orange lining. It's bright orange, too."

"Thanks," Rusty said as he pulled the door open.

"She's helping with the angels in the pageant," Renee offered. She couldn't seem to let him step through the door. She found herself wanting to pull him back. "If you need to talk to her, she'll be there tonight."

Rusty nodded. "Thanks."

And then he was gone.

The room was suddenly cold and she felt a shiver inside. She walked over to the fireplace and took a minute to check Tessie's coloring. The girl wasn't as enthusiastic as usual. Renee knew she couldn't have heard her conversation with Rusty, but Tessie picked up on emotions.

This Christmas had started out with such promise, Renee thought to herself, and then it slid downhill. She had just escaped a marriage with a criminal, though, and she'd never again marry a man who broke the law. Not even if she loved him more than she thought possible and he made her daughter laugh.

But had Rusty done anything wrong? She was coming to believe he hadn't.

Rusty borrowed a ranch pickup in the afternoon and drove over to his childhood home, hoping he would find some clue as to what was going on there. The barn was as he had left it when he put his duffel in the hayloft some days ago. The house was unlocked and, apart from a layer of dust, hadn't changed in years. He stopped in the living room to wind the grandfather clock that had stood in the house for the past two generations. It started right up, marking the passage of every minute Rusty stood there.

Then he climbed the stairs to the bedrooms, checking in Eric's first to see if there was any sign of the boy. He'd been there recently, if the scatter of clothes was to be believed.

Rusty's old bedroom was the way he'd left it eight years ago, right down to the plastic curtains someone had put on the windows for him. They were not white any longer, but the swirled pattern remained.

His father's room had been cleared out, except for the bed and dresser. Rusty felt a moment's pang imagining his younger brother needing to take care of the man's belongings after he died. Rusty had been on a deep-cover mission in Afghanistan at the time of his father's death and hadn't even heard about his funeral until it was over. He'd called and talked to Eric as soon as he could, making arrangements for the boy to stay with the Morgans until Rusty could come home.

At the time, he could have taken a trip back for a week or so to spend with his brother, but since he'd be getting out of the service in a few months, it hadn't seemed necessary. Now Rusty regretted not doing it.

Sometimes it seemed his life was one misstep after another, he thought. He shouldn't have pressed Renee this morning on her feelings about him, not when he hadn't even figured out himself what was going on.

And the sad truth was that he might never know. He was innocent, so he knew there'd never be anything but circumstantial evidence that he was involved with the rustling around here. But unless the truth was discovered, people would always wonder if he'd had something to do with it.

As long as there was any doubt, he needed to stay away from Renee and Tessie. He did not want to force Renee to know the agony of choosing between him and the new life she was building for herself and her daughter. She wasn't convinced of his innocence, even yet.

Rusty had to stay in the area until everything was resolved with the rustling. The sheriff had been helpful with that. The lawman had said he'd already asked the Havre sheriff's department to try to find a contact for the corporation that had purchased the Calhoun family ranch. Maybe he and Eric could stay in the house until they found another place. It seemed a small thing to ask since no one was living in it yet.

After walking through some of the fields, Rusty decided it was time to drive into Dry Creek so he could help get everything set up for the pageant that night. He was surprised at how attached he'd become to the whole community here. His family had always held themselves apart from the rest of the people in the area. Rusty told himself that if he ever lived here again, he would be part of everything. Even if it meant wearing a lacy purple robe to play King Herod in the pageant.

Chapter Twelve

Renee tied Tessie's blond curls back with a white ribbon. The girl was wearing her red dress to the pageant and she'd change into her angel robe and wings once she got there. Renee had already put some new glitter on Tessie's angel wings.

"Is Rusty going?" Tessie asked for the second time in the past hour.

"Yes, sweetie," Renee answered. "I hope so."

The man better show up, she told herself. He hadn't stopped by the bunkhouse for the early supper she'd served the ranch hands. Not that he had to come, of course. He had told Pete he was going over to his family's old ranch to look around, but Renee couldn't help thinking how easy it would be for him to just drive down to the highway and head east. Or north or south. He could lose himself in some distant place and never have to worry about the crimes being committed around Dry Creek—or any part he'd had in them.

Renee looked up as she and Tessie walked out to the pickup. The dark sky was clear and she could see a sprinkling of stars. It had snowed all week but the temperature had been high enough at times yesterday and today to melt most of the snow that was on the ground. They might not have a white Christmas after all.

Dozens of pickups and a few cars were parked outside the barn when Renee pulled in. If it had been light out, she would have looked for the pickup Rusty had borrowed, but in the night all she saw were dark shapes that looked alike.

She could identify the pickup with the horse trailer as the one Eric and Karyn had borrowed to bring their donkey to the pageant. The braying told her the donkey had not yet been unloaded.

Renee held Tessie's hand as they walked toward the barn. She was glad her daughter was excited about the evening. When she opened the door, a burst of light and laughter stood before them.

They stepped in and Tessie took off. That was enough unlike her daughter that Renee followed. The girl was unerring in her path and she ended up standing at Rusty's feet.

"Did you bring the crown I made you?" Tessie demanded from where she stood with her hands on her hips. "A king needs a crown!"

Rusty smiled down at the girl. "I sure did."

He reached behind him and brought back a brown paper grocery bag, the kind she kept stacked in a corner of the bunkhouse for everyday use. He opened it and pulled out a paper crown, cut out from the same paper as the bag. Someone, and it had to be Tessie, had colored jewels all over the crown.

Rusty put the handmade creation on his head and it fit.

"The best crown a king ever had," he said to Tessie as he made a slight bow.

Tessie stared at him as if he were a real king. "It's beautiful."

Renee felt useless. She should have thought of the crown. Well, she had thought of it earlier, but with all that had happened lately, she had forgotten.

"It does look nice," Renee said, giving a smile to her daughter. "I love the colors you used."

Tessie had used some of her special glitter crayons so the reds shone deep and the yellows sparkled like real gems. The crown had a series of points and each point had a shimmering green circle on it like an emerald.

"They're king colors," Tessie agreed.

Just then Mrs. Hargrove came through with a clipboard in her hand saying, "Costumes, everyone. Put your costumes on." She stopped and looked at Rusty. "Where's your robe?"

Rusty reached to a chair beside him and pulled up the shiny purple robe. "Here."

He looked at Renee for a moment and she almost laughed.

"It's not so bad," she murmured, holding back a chuckle.

"Not if you're a Vegas showgirl," Rusty said as he put the robe on. He'd obviously practiced, because he did it very quickly for a man with his arm in a sling.

When he was finished, he asked, "So, how do I look?"

"Nice crown," Mrs. Hargrove said before she hurried away.

"You look beautiful," Tessie repeated.

Renee found herself staring at Rusty. How could a man with so much goodwill and humor steal from anyone?

Before long, the call came for the angels to line up behind the bleachers, so Renee guided Tessie to the right place. Rusty needed to get set up for the first scene with the wise men. The actors portrayed that encounter while Joseph led the donkey that carried Mary in the background.

Rusty stood behind one set of bleachers. He'd just made a second trip to the coatracks, looking for any signs of an orange parka. The one with an orange lining did belong to a girl, just as Renee had said. While he was standing there, she came in wearing the parka and hung it up on the hooks. Since she had a Christmas brooch on the parka, he figured it couldn't belong to any man. So he went back to the place where he was to wait behind the bleachers.

By the time he got back, the wise men were there, too. They were all going to walk out when the narrator started telling the story of the birth of Jesus.

"Cool crown," one of the pint-size wise men said a little sarcastically.

Rusty turned to look at the young teenager. The boy had a maroon velvet robe on with gold piping all around it. A gold-foil-wrapped box was in his hands.

Rusty gave the boy his mean look. "The crown's beautiful."

The boy looked suitably chastised. "Yes, sir."

It was quiet after that for a minute.

"Did you really try to murder the baby Jesus?" one of the other boys asked. His box was silver and his robe was black, but he looked like the other wise man.

"I'm an actor," Rusty said. "Actors don't murder anyone."

Well, that might be an overstatement of fact, Rusty told himself, but it got his point across. At least there were no other remarks.

The lights dimmed in the barn and instrumental music came from the sound system. The chorus of little angels began singing "Silent Night." Rusty walked over to the edge of the bleachers so he could see Tessie sing. Her wings were crooked, but her face was full of joy.

After the song, Joseph started leading the donkey across the stage area. Mary was seated on top of the animal, her blue cotton robe covering her. Rusty noticed his brother was having a hard time getting the donkey to maintain a steady pace. The beast was a little spooked by the lights in the barn and throwing its head around as if it wanted to be free of its burden. Fortunately, Joseph had enough sense to stop and help Mary down from the donkey, then they continued on their way. The plan was that Mary would wait behind the far bleachers while Joseph, or Eric, took the donkey back out to the horse trailer.

The narrator started and the wise men were on the move.

Rusty stood in his King Herod robe and faced the audience. He glared at as many of the audience members as he could, being careful not to let his stare rest too long on any one person so that no one would misunderstand and think it was personal.

Well, he did swing his gaze over to where the shepherds were peeking out from the opposite set of bleachers, but all they did was grin and give him a thumbs-up.

Before he knew it, the wise men were in front of him, asking their questions and telling their story.

"Come back to see me," he finally said, his voice full and strong. "I'd like to visit this child, too, and pay my respects."

The wise men left after that and Rusty turned to walk back to the bleachers.

He heard something that stopped him. He didn't know how he heard it with all the shuffling of feet as the shepherds prepared to come and be startled by the main angel. But he did.

It was the ping of a bullet hitting a piece of tin outside. It wasn't loud. The gun must have had a silencer on it, but he had heard bullets too many times to be mistaken.

"Everybody stay inside!" Rusty yelled as he started for the door closest to the sound. "Turn the lights off and get behind the bleachers."

People were stunned for a moment and then chaos broke loose. Fortunately, the sheriff was running toward the same door as Rusty and they met just before going outside.

"I'll go left," Rusty said.

"I'll go right," the sheriff said as he pulled out a gun from a shoulder holster and handed it to Rusty. He then pulled his service revolver from the holster at his hip. "Don't shoot the guy if you can help it."

Rusty nodded. He didn't want to think how many permit laws they were breaking, but he was glad the sheriff wasn't willing to send an unarmed man out to catch someone with a gun.

When Rusty turned left, the first thing he saw was the donkey standing outside of the horse trailer, tossing its head and getting ready to kick.

The parked vehicles made good cover as Rusty worked his way over to the trailer. His brother hadn't answered, but that might be best if someone was looking for a target.

Father God, help me, Rusty prayed, surprising even himself. The chaplain had shown him how to start and now it was like a flood pouring out of him. *Keep my brother safe, God. Just keep him safe.*

Rusty felt his spirit lighten as he drew closer to the donkey. Maybe God did listen to someone like him after all.

When Rusty passed the last pickup between him and the trailer, he saw a dark shape under the horse trailer. He could tell the figure was wearing a robe and for a moment he thought Eric might have been shot. Then the shape moved.

A shot rang out on the other side of the parked vehicles, but Rusty bent down to look under the trailer.

"Stay away from that donkey," Eric hissed from where he hid. "He almost killed me, kicking at me and carrying on. If I hadn't gotten under here, I'd be dead."

"I suspect someone was shooting at him," Rusty said as he looked back to where the other shots had come from.

If it wasn't for the silencer on the gun, Rusty would think it was vandals having their fun shooting up the vehicles at the church pageant. But a silencer meant it was someone on a more serious mission.

A second shot sounded, followed by a scream.

"I got him!" the sheriff shouted.

Rusty ran back through the parked vehicles until he saw the sheriff standing at the edge of the road, just past where people had parked.

Rusty saw a man lying on the ground in front of the lawman. He could hear the man cursing, so he knew the sheriff had only wounded him.

"Look who we have here," the sheriff said to Rusty as he approached.

Rusty looked down and saw a man in an orange parka trying to sit up even though he had what looked like a shoulder wound. Then he stepped closer so he could see the man's face.

"Otis?" Rusty said in astonishment. His father's friend. The bank employee. "What are you doing here?"

No one bothered answering the question and Rusty knew. He'd just never suspected Otis.

"Well, this sheds more light on this whole thing," the sheriff said.

By that time Eric had crawled out from under the trailer and walked over, too.

"Is this the man?" Rusty asked his brother, still not believing the obvious.

Eric nodded. "He doesn't look so scary now."

Otis growled and tried harder to stand. Finally, he began to shout, "Don't you turn me in, you little weasel! I can still get you from prison. I know people. I said I'd hurt you if you talked and I will."

"Did Eric have anything to do with your rustling?" the sheriff asked.

Otis snorted. "Who, him? No. The kid is worthless. I'd never partner up with the likes of him."

"Who would you partner up with?" Rusty asked.

Otis clamped his lips tight on that question, but Rusty figured the circle of rustlers was likely to include some connection to Denny Hampton.

A couple of men from inside the barn had come out by now and the sheriff sent one to call for an ambulance, then told everyone to go inside and finish the pageant. The children had worked hard and it wasn't fair to hold it up over some thief who should have known better.

Rusty took his brother inside and was proud when Eric merely went over to wait with Karyn for their next cue as Joseph and Mary. His brother was going to carry on.

As for himself, Rusty searched the scared faces in the bleachers until he found Renee. He might not be welcome in her life, but he needed to assure her that everything was safe now.

She was in the back bleachers and she slid over to make a space as soon as she saw him. Few sat up this high and they all leaned against the barn wall.

"Are you all right?" she whispered. She put her hand on his arm. "You didn't hurt your shoulder again, did you?"

He shook his head. "I'm just fine. The sheriff is out there arresting the man in the orange parka."

"The one Eric wouldn't identify?"

"The very one," Rusty assured her.

'Who was it?"

"Otis. From the bank."

"So you're not a suspect?" Renee asked and Rusty could see the change in her eyes.

"Not anymore."

Mrs. Hargrove picked up a microphone and told everyone they were safe and a full report of the happenings outside would be made after the pageant was over. Then the shepherds filed out and began to sing "Hark, the Herald Angels Sing."

It was a challenging song for the shepherds, Rusty thought, but they manfully tried to hit the high notes.

By the second verse, he'd put his arm around Renee. She turned to him and smiled. Hidden as they were back here, he was tempted to kiss her, but he saw the shepherds eyeing him.

"The sheriff wants to talk to me and Eric after the pageant," Rusty said as the shepherds struggled with a note. "But I want to ask if I can spend some time tomorrow with you and Tessie."

Renee nodded. Her eyes were shining. "That would be good."

He had never seen anyone so beautiful. The pearl coloring he'd seen in her when he was practically unconscious was still there. Her skin shimmered. Her eyes sparkled with happiness.

Rusty forgot about the shepherds. He leaned over and kissed her. A sound swept over him that must have been the shepherds' astonishment at the angel. Rusty figured he knew how they felt. Some things in life were beyond expression.

He pulled away finally, wondering if his eyes were as dazed as hers.

"Tomorrow," he said with promise.

Mrs. Hargrove explained what had happened in the parking lot. The rest of the pageant passed in a blur and before he knew it, people were streaming out of the barn and into the parking area. Rusty walked over to Eric, and the brothers went together to meet with the sheriff.

Tomorrow would be a better day, Rusty promised himself. He'd spend it with Renee without the cloud of suspicion over him. Anything was possible now.

Chapter Thirteen

Flurries of snow were falling the next morning. It was barely light as Renee lay in bed and watched the tiny flakes float down from the sky. Frost outlined the windows and the air was cold. It was going to be a white Christmas—a new beginning for her and Tessie.

She was already humming a song. She planned to put a CD of old-fashioned carols on the Elktons' surround-sound system when she got up and lit the fireplace in the living room.

Renee planned to sneak out of bed and bring hot chocolate back for Tessie as a special treat, but she got only one step toward the door before the girl rolled over in bed.

"Is it Christmas?" Tessie whispered.

Renee nodded. The girl's eyes were excited and Renee motioned for her to come.

They had agreed to wait to open most of their presents until Rusty could be with them. He was coming over at ten o'clock. But Renee had promised her daughter she could go to her stocking on the fireplace and see her present from Santa the very first thing.

When Tessie stepped into the hall, she raced for her stocking. Renee didn't even try to keep up.

"It's me!" the girl screamed as Renee turned the corner into the room.

The doll was almost as tall as Tessie, and Renee had picked out the hair and eye colors so they would look like her daughter's. Then she'd taken some remnants of material from the pajamas she'd sewn for Tessie a month before and made an identical pair for her doll. She'd done the same with the red dress Tessie loved so much.

The girl would have played with her new Me Doll all morning, but Renee reminded her that they needed to go wish the ranch hands a merry Christmas and feed them breakfast. Tessie clapped her hands and asked what they would eat.

Before going to bed, Renee had made two large French-toast casseroles and refrigerated them. Then she'd pulled some special brown-sugar-and-peppercorn-crusted bacon from the freezer to go with the casserole. They'd have orange juice and coffee. Then about one o'clock they'd have a ham-and-sweet-potato dinner.

When they got to the bunkhouse, Renee expected Rusty to be there. She decided he must be getting some extra sleep. But when he still wasn't around when she brought the hot French toast to the table, she asked Pete.

"Oh, he went Christmas shopping," Pete said as if it was the most natural thing in the world.

"Today?" Renee was dismayed. There wasn't a store open anywhere in Dry Creek. He would have had to go into Billings, and that would take all day.

Pete shrugged. "That's what he said."

Renee wished she hadn't already told Tessie he was coming. It was eight o'clock; there was no way he'd be back by ten.

Tessie would have been excited to see him any day, but today she would also be impatient to open her presents.

Renee was finished with the dishes and back at the main house by nine. She'd decided they'd still open presents at ten even though Rusty might not be there.

The hour passed pleasantly. Renee watched Tessie play with her doll. They took a break and had some hot chocolate. They swung their arms around as they sang "Jingle Bell Rock" together with the CD.

The doorbell rang at two minutes to ten. Renee hadn't heard a vehicle drive up, so she thought it must be Pete with a phone message from Rusty saying he wouldn't be coming after all. She had her fake smile in place so she could assure him that everything was fine.

But when she opened the door, Rusty stood there. He had a large brown coat draped over his shoulders and the sling he wore on his injured arm seemed to have grown huge.

Her smile turned to the real thing. "You made it."

She stepped aside so he could come in. "I thought you were out Christmas shopping."

He grinned as he stomped his feet on the mat in front of the door. "I was."

"But nothing's open!"

"The best presents don't come from stores," Rusty said as he continued to stand, his eyes searching over her shoulder.

Tessie came running out of the living room and didn't stop until she was at the feet of her prince.

"I've got presents!" the girl declared gleefully. "Four of them. One from Mommy. One from Grandpa. One from Mrs. Hargrove. And one from Pete."

"She's read all the labels," Renee said.

"I don't think that can be right," Rusty said, his voice serious.

"I counted," Tessie said firmly and held up four fingers.

"But you have one more," Rusty said as he knelt down so he was level with Tessie.

The girl screeched in excitement as she saw the furry black-and-white head peek out from the front of Rusty's coat.

"A puppy! You got me a puppy!"

Rusty nodded and looked up at Renee. "I know you didn't have time. And if the two of you want one of the other puppies in the litter instead, you can exchange her. Or we can look for a different puppy altogether."

Tessie was already pulling the puppy out of Rusty's coat and cooing over her as if she was the best puppy she'd ever seen.

"I better not let Dog see this," Rusty said to Renee when Tessie raced down the hall chasing her new pet. "He'll be jealous."

"Come sit down," Renee said. "I don't think Tessie is going to be ready to open the rest of her presents for some time. I can fix you some coffee or hot chocolate."

The snow accumulated on the ground in the next hour as Tessie played with her new puppy and Renee and Rusty sat by the fire talking. He told her that the sheriff had called him this morning to say that he'd talked to the bank in Havre that had held the mortgage on his family farm, the loan that Otis had overseen. Apparently Otis had stolen the money when Rusty's father had given him enough to pay off the loan. The money had only made Otis greedy, though, and that was when he'd set up the rustling ring. The sheriff said the Calhoun ranch would be given back to the brothers as soon as new documents could be signed.

"So I'll have a home again," Rusty said, his voice taking on a shy note. "Eric will live with me some, but he's said he wants to go to college next year."

"That's wonderful," Renee said.

They both sipped their cups of hot chocolate and were silent for a minute.

"I have a present for you," Rusty said then.

"Another puppy?" Renee teased. She couldn't think what other presents could be found locally on Christmas Day.

He shook his head and pulled a small tissue-wrapped package from this coat pocket. He held it out to her.

Renee accepted it curiously. The gift was tied with a red ribbon. It was light, no bigger than a paperback book. But it was bumpy instead of firmly rectangular.

"Open it," Rusty urged her.

Renee untied the ribbon and the tissue fell away.

"Oh," she breathed.

A strand of perfect pearls lay in her hand. The gems shimmered in the overhead light and they felt warm to her touch.

Then she realized. "This isn't the necklace you got for your mother so long ago?"

He nodded. "I've carried it with me for eight years and slept with it under my pillow before that. I've loved it and hated it. But it's had a place in my heart all that time and I want you to have it."

Renee looked at him closely to see if he really meant to give away something so important to him, but she couldn't focus with the tears in her eyes.

"You're sure?"

"Never more sure of anything," Rusty said, his voice thick with emotion. "I know I'll let you down sometimes. I'm learning we all fail each other now and again. You may have to forgive me and I may have to forgive you. With God's help we can do that. I love you and I can't imagine living my life with anyone else."

"I—" Renee started to say. She hadn't trusted him. Could he forgive her for that?

"I know it's too soon," Rusty added. "You want to be cautious. I understand that. But I want you to know I will be around, and when you're ready, I'm going to propose marriage to you."

"But—" Renee began again.

"I know," Rusty said. "You need to be sure. And I agree. Take all the time you want to make up your mind."

Renee held up her hand in a stop gesture.

"What I'm trying to say is that I hung on to my suspicions longer than I should have. I'm not sure it's fair to you—"

His face fell. "You're looking for a way out?"

"No," she said. "I'm already starting to love you. I just need to work on trusting my feelings."

"Well," Rusty said as his smile grew. "We can work on that."

Then he leaned down. Renee stretched closer. Their lips met.

Renee vaguely wondered if a kiss was supposed to be this sweet. Then she didn't think about anything. She just let her emotions guide her heart. She had found her love.

* * * * *

Dear Reader,

Thank you for visiting the small town of Dry Creek with me. As always, I think of readers like you when I write.

In this book I tell Renee's story. She's the daughter of Calen Gray from *Second Chance in Dry Creek*. I wanted to give her more story, as I had wondered what would happen to her and her young daughter, Tessie. It isn't easy to make a new life for oneself and that's what Renee had to do.

I know some of you have had to rebuild shattered lives, too, so I will pass along the tip that made it all better for Renee. She found a church and drew close to the people there. I recommend the same for you.

If you have some time, drop me a line and let me know you enjoy the series. You can contact me through my website at www.janettronstad.com.

Sincerely yours,

Janet Tronstad

Questions for Discussion

1. Renee was afraid because of her abusive relationship with her ex-husband. She let that fear stop her from getting close to other men. What would you say to Renee if you could talk to her in the beginning of the book?

2. Renee didn't really want to open her home to a strange man, even if he was in desperate need of help. Has God ever called you to do something you really didn't want to do? What happened?

3. Renee's little girl, Tessie, insisted the strange man who was unconscious on their porch was a prince. Do you think there is a place in the life of a child for fantasies (fairy tales, Santa)? Why or why not?

4. Tessie's fantasies helped her to deal with her ambivalent feelings toward her father. What helps you cope with confused feelings? Are there any Bible verses that give you comfort during these times?

5. Betty, the dispatcher for the sheriff, wanted to find a match for Renee, in part because Tessie needed a new father. Betty tried encouraging Renee to date and said she'd set her up with someone if Renee wanted. What do you think are some good matchmaking steps: prayer, encouragement, inviting potential mates to the same event, setting up a blind date?

6. Rusty felt responsible for others and guilty when things went wrong. Have you ever felt this way? What Bible verses would you give to Rusty if you could talk to him?

7. Rusty and Renee both felt there were things God just couldn't forgive because they couldn't forgive them. Do you believe there are sins too big for God to forgive? What are they? What does the Bible say about unforgivable sin?

8. Renee had moved around a lot with her ex-husband and was determined to make Dry Creek her home. The church was a big part of what drew her to the community. What do you think makes a church welcoming to others? Do you belong to a church like that?

COMING NEXT MONTH FROM
Love Inspired®

Available October 22, 2013

TAIL OF TWO HEARTS
The Heart of Main Street • by Charlotte Carter

Pet-store owner Chase Rollins never saw himself as a family man. Can Vivian Duncan convince him to open his heart to her—and her baby—so they can build a future together?

REBECCA'S CHRISTMAS GIFT
Hannah's Daughters • by Emma Miller

Rebecca agrees to keep house for widowed preacher Caleb Wittner for the holidays—but never expects to fall in love with this man and his charming daughter.

THE FIREFIGHTER'S MATCH
Gordon Falls • by Allie Pleiter

As Gordon Falls' first female firefighter, Josephine Jones knows how to protect herself from getting burned, but can she protect her heart from the dashing adventurer who's trying to steal it?

YULETIDE TWINS
by Renee Andrews

Alone and pregnant, Laura Holland needs a friend and a job. When she turns to David Presley, she realizes the friendship she's always counted on could be the love she's always wished for.

SLEIGH BELL SWEETHEARTS
by Teri Wilson

Alaskan pilot Zoey Hathaway is in for the Christmas of her life when she inherits a reindeer farm...and one brooding, dangerously attractive ranch hand.

SEASON OF HOPE
by Virginia Carmichael

To help his community, Gavin Sawyer agrees to work with the Denver Mission. What he doesn't bargain for is falling for fellow volunteer Evie Thorne.

LOOK FOR THESE AND OTHER LOVE INSPIRED BOOKS WHEREVER BOOKS ARE SOLD, INCLUDING MOST BOOKSTORES, SUPERMARKETS, DISCOUNT STORES AND DRUGSTORES.

LICNM1013

REQUEST YOUR FREE BOOKS!

2 FREE INSPIRATIONAL NOVELS
PLUS 2
FREE
MYSTERY GIFTS

Love Inspired

A shy bookstore employee runs into her youthful crush.

Read on for a sneak preview of
TAIL OF TWO HEARTS
by Charlotte Carter, the next book in
THE HEART OF MAIN STREET series,
available November 2013.

Vivian Duncan stepped out of Happy Endings Bookstore onto the sidewalk in the small Kansas town of Bygones. Watching leaves and bits of paper racing down the street, blown by a brisk breeze, she inhaled the crisp November air.

She hoped the owner of Fluff & Stuff, Chase Rollins, would help her put together a special event at the bookstore to promote books about dogs.

As she opened the door, the big green-cheeked parrot near the cash register squawked his greeting, "What's up? What's up?" He proudly bobbed his head and did a little dance on his perch.

"Hello, Pepper." Vivian smiled at Chase's recently acquired bird that was looking for a new home.

"Good birdie! Good birdie!" he vocalized.

"I'm sure you are." She looked around for Chase.

His warm brown eyes lit up when he spotted Vivian, and he produced a delighted smile. "Hey, Viv."

Smiling, he stepped toward Vivian. When she'd first met him, she'd thought he was an attractive man. She still did. At six foot two with a muscular body, he towered over her five-foot-four frame, even when she was wearing heels. His short, dark hair had a natural wave that sculpted his head. His nose was straight, his lips nicely full.

"What can I do for you?" he asked.

"I, uh…" Snapping back from her train of thought, she started over. "Allison at Happy Endings and I have realized books about dogs are particularly popular. We'd like to put on some sort of a special event and thought you could give us some guidance about where to get a dog or two for show-and-tell. I know the puppies you have are from the local shelter."

Chase ignored the bird. "The shelter is getting over-crowded, so I've started a monthly Adopt a Pet Day here at the shop. In fact I'm having one this Saturday." He handed her a flyer from the stack on the counter. "And I'd love to help you with your event."

"I'm glad." She was relieved, too, that Chase could help out.

"When you visit the shelter you'll have to be careful not to fall in love." His eyes twinkled, and his lively grin was pure temptation.

Vivian blinked. Her cheeks flushed. Had he said *fall in love?*

Pick up TAIL OF TWO HEARTS
wherever Love Inspired® books are sold.

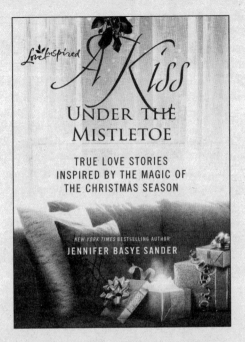

Christmas has a way of reminding us of what really matters—and what could be more important than our loved ones? From husbands and wives to boyfriends and girlfriends to long-lost loves, the real-life romances in this book are surrounded by the joy and blessings of the Christmas season.

Featuring stories by favorite Love Inspired authors, this collection will warm your heart and soothe your soul through the long winter. *A Kiss Under the Mistletoe* beautifully celebrates the way love and faith can transform a cold day in December into the most magical day of the year.

On sale October 29!

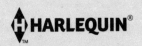

During the Christmas season, Rebecca Yoder agrees to help new preacher Caleb Wittner with his mischievous daughter. Amelia's turned the community of Seven Poplars upside down. Only Rebecca can see the pain hidden beneath the little girl's antics—and her father's brusque manner. After losing his wife in a fire, Caleb's physical scars may be healing, but his emotions have not. Yet Rebecca's sweet manner soon has him smiling and laughing with his daughter—and his pretty housekeeper. Soon Caleb must decide whether to invite Rebecca into his life—or lose her forever.

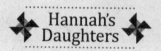

Hannah's Daughters

Rebecca's Christmas Gift

by

Emma Miller

Available November 2013
wherever Love Inspired books are sold.

Find us on Facebook at
www.Facebook.com/LoveInspiredBooks

www.Harlequin.com

LI87848